LOVE ME TENDER, LOVE YOU HARD

(Cookin' With SEALs #1)

SHARON HAMILTON

SHARON HAMILTON'S BOOK LIST

SEAL BROTHERHOOD BOOKS

SEAL BROTHERHOOD SERIES
Accidental SEAL Book 1
Fallen SEAL Legacy Book 2
SEAL Under Covers Book 3
SEAL The Deal Book 4
Cruisin' For A SEAL Book 5
SEAL My Destiny Book 6
SEAL of My Heart Book 7
Fredo's Dream Book 8
SEAL My Love Book 9
SEAL Encounter Prequel to Book 1
SEAL Endeavor Prequel to Book 2
Ultimate SEAL Collection Vol. 1 Books 1-4 /2 Prequels
Ultimate SEAL Collection Vol. 2 Books 5-7

BAD BOYS OF SEAL TEAM 3 SERIES
SEAL's Promise Book 1
SEAL My Home Book 2
SEAL's Code Book 3
Big Bad Boys Bundle Books 1-3

BAND OF BACHELORS SERIES
Lucas Book 1
Alex Book 2
Jake Book 3

Jake 2 Book 4

Big Band of Bachelors Bundle

BONE FROG BROTHERHOOD SERIES

New Year's SEAL Dream Book 1

SEALed At The Altar Book 2

SEALed Forever Book 3

SEAL's Rescue Book 4

SEALed Protection Book 5

SILVER SEALS SERIES

SEAL Love's Legacy

SLEEPER SEALS SERIES

Bachelor SEAL

SUNSET SEALS SERIES

SEALed at Sunset

Second Chance SEAL

Treasure Island SEAL

Escape to Sunset

STAND ALONE BOOKS & SERIES

SEAL's Goal: The Beautiful Game

Nashville SEAL: Jameson

True Blue SEALS Zak

Paradise: In Search of Love

Love Me Tender, Love You Hard

NOVELLAS

SEAL You In My Dreams Magnolias and Moonshine

PARANORMALS

GOLDEN VAMPIRES OF TUSCANY SERIES
Honeymoon Bite Book 1
Mortal Bite Book 2
Christmas Bite Book 3
Midnight Bite Book 4

THE GUARDIANS
Heavenly Lover Book 1
Underworld Lover Book 2
Underworld Queen Book 3

FALL FROM GRACE SERIES
Gideon: Heavenly Fall

NOVELLAS
SEAL Of Time Trident Legacy

All of Sharon's books are available on Audible,
narrated by the talented J.D. Hart.

AUTHOR'S NOTE

I always dedicate my SEAL Brotherhood books to the brave men and women who defend our shores and keep us safe. Without their sacrifice, and that of their families—because a warrior's fight always includes his or her family—I wouldn't have the freedom and opportunity to make a living writing these stories. They sometimes pay the ultimate price so we can debate, argue, go have coffee with friends, raise our children and see them have children of their own.

One of my favorite tributes to warriors resides on many memorials, including one I saw honoring the fallen of WWII on an island in the Pacific:

> "When you go home
> Tell them of us, and say
> For your tomorrow,
> We gave our today."

These are my stories created out of my own imagination. Anything that is inaccurately portrayed is either my mistake, or done intentionally to disguise something I might have overheard over a beer or in the corner of one of the hangouts along the Coronado Strand.

I support two main charities. Navy SEAL/UDT Museum operates in Ft. Pierce, Florida. Please learn about this wonderful museum, all run by active and former SEALs and their friends and families, and who rely on public support, not that of the U.S. Government. www.navysealmuseum.org

IF YOU GOT ANY CLOSER, YOU WOULD HAVE TO ENLIST

I also support Wounded Warriors, who tirelessly bring together the warrior as well as the family members who are just learning to deal with their soldier's condition and have nowhere to turn. It is a long path to becoming well, but I've seen first-hand what this organization does for its warriors and the families who love them. Please give what your heart tells you is right. If you cannot give, volunteer at one of the many service centers all over the United States. Get involved. Do something meaningful for someone who gave so much of themselves, to families who have paid the price for your freedom. You'll find a family there unlike any other on the planet.

www.woundedwarriorproject.org

CHAPTER 1

FORMER SEAL DEREK Farley was having a bad week. The call at midnight rattled him more than he wanted to admit. He believed he was completely over Remy. But when his friend said she was spotted in a white uniform in St. Helena, it got his mind going. He couldn't get past the idea of what she might look like all dressed up like a gothic nurse—her hair mussed like they'd just tussled in the sheets. It scared him how much he missed her. How he thought about her nearly twenty-four-seven. Not that he'd admit it to anyone, especially Knudsen, his former teammate from SEAL Team 5.

He assumed the dreams and fantasies would subside now that sixty days had gone by.

He was dead wrong.

No way Remington Bolt would become a nurse, he'd said over the phone.

"Well," Knudsen began in his mock southern

drawl, "she was *definitely* in white. And she wasn't a bride, if that's what you are worried about." His comment ended with a low growl.

Derek winced. "I'm not worried about that," he lied.

"Sure. Well, I just thought you ought to know. You were wondering where she took off to."

He never should have brought it up, and now Knudsen wasn't convinced of his lack of interest. The guy had to know he'd been trying, *really* trying to get her out of his mind. But she was there, and no amount of eye or brain bleach would remove her. All he could think about was Remington and the way she held a semi-automatic. How those fingers slid over the shaft of his long guns as she fondled them the way she had no right to. How she looked in the shower, her backside all silky and wet, that little *come on in* twinkle in her eye as she sucked a finger and showed him right where he should focus.

He even loved perusing her body while she made him breakfast, as she liked to do naked on those long, lazy mornings in San Diego. Sometimes he wouldn't let her finish, and so he'd eaten a lot of cold breakfasts over the months they were together.

One by one, the days whirled before his eyes, images of times before his last deployment and injury recovery, back when he used to laugh a lot. Well, maybe not a lot, but a whole lot more than he did these days, drunk or sober. Any one of those sexy images was ripe for the cover of a men's health magazine and could qualify as a Viagra alternative. He'd been lonely these past sixty days, but he'd been hard as a rock, too.

"Derek, you still there, buddy?" Knudsen's voice crackled and forced Derek's brain through the sieve of reality he called "Missing Remy." Except he didn't dare call it that to anyone. Not even to himself.

From the reality of his cold, lonely bed in his tiny apartment that was even more tiny since she'd left, the postage stamp view of the ocean now unremarkable, he mumbled, trying to biff off the stiffy that defied him still. "So where did you say you spotted her?" His voice croaked just like in high school when he couldn't speak around pretty girls. If the pressure between his legs didn't stop, he'd have to roll over on himself or dump a glass of water on his crotch.

"At Mayberry's. She was fondling melons, and, well, Derek, that was one helluva—"

"Shut the fuck up." It was none of his business what Remington looked like holding cantaloupes in her palms. He knew full well what her own enormous melons looked like, tasted like in the flesh. That was part of the problem. And it didn't help his concentration, but rather sent it directly south. What he'd done with those melons on hundreds of occasions defied logic and the laws of space and time. Now he'd *never* get back to bed. He had to get rid of Knudsen before he did or said something he'd regret.

"Well, Remington has her future ahead of her, and I have mine. But thanks for telling me. Next time, don't call me at midnight."

"Sure, Derek. So we got another thirty days before we start workup. San Diego's cool, but up here? You'd love it. When are you gonna to join me? We'd have a blast. Town's nice. Girls are pretty, although not a lot of them, not like San Diego. You could make it look like you weren't spying on her."

Derek hadn't told anyone about being dumped from the Teams. There would be no workup for him. He'd need to have that conversation soon with Knudsen. Maybe today.

But his main objection right now was he didn't want to admit he'd been to St. Helena before. With Remington. A nice—*very* nice—weekend there at a bed and breakfast. But for them, it was mostly just the bed part that mattered.

He didn't have to see Knudsen's face. He could feel the former Teammate's smile and suspected his teeth still had remnants of dinner stuffed between their pearly rows. Horse teeth. Knudsen and his whole family had big, white horse teeth as hard and big as a real horse. He wondered how he ever kissed a girl without those teeth getting in the way.

Derek was stalling for the answer he didn't want to give, but knew he would.

Oh shit, here it comes. He felt the constriction in his chest, his stomach, and, yes, in his balls.

His mind manufactured the long, painfully piercing scream from the House of Horrors, and Derek knew Knudsen was enjoying the moment tremendously. They'd spent so much time together in combat they knew each other's inner secrets and thoughts just as if they were married, except neither of them were. Both confirmed bachelors, talk was cheap and stories were honest when you were waiting for action and preparing to meet your maker in a country you didn't even like. Giving his life away for pennies.

Not that it made any difference. Being dead was being dead. Didn't mean Jack what your bank account had in it if you were dead. Or how much they paid you or your survivors to do it.

But something about Remington going on and having a life without him really disturbed him. His head screamed like the first and only time he'd been to a heavy metal concert. It wasn't his ears hurting. No, his abused heart felt like it had been tied up in barbed wire, discarded, hung by a meat hook, and tossed over the telephone wire down by the only stop sign in his home town of Deganville.

Sonofabitch.

"Talk to me, Derek. I'm a good listener."

Well, wasn't that special? Now Knudsen sounded like a goddamned counselor, one of those the Navy sent him to now that they'd dropped him from the Teams.

"I'm thinking," he said, stalling for time.

Knudsen chuckled and then rubbed it in really good, just for effect, "Well, you know what you always told me. *'Thinking's a luxury in the war zone. If you gotta think, your training sucked.'*"

"Except this is no fucking war zone. Would you quit it and give me a moment?"

Undeterred, Knudsen continued, "…And her training sucked. Sucked you real good."

"Fuck you."

"Sure, man."

Derek knew Knudsen was beginning to show restraint. He didn't sigh all pissy like he wanted to. He waited. The guy knew him well. Derek took a deep breath and held it as long as he could, exhaling slowly without making a sound. It began to work.

Well, he'd not been a saint either, but she'd partied all night with his now ex-best friend—a newbie guy on one of the other SEAL teams the night before Ray's first deployment. She called it a *send-off.* He could imagine what kind of a send-off she gave the little frog all right. Ray was probably still dreaming about her—

licking his lips and fondling himself.

Just like Derek was. He inhaled and punched his pillow. He couldn't speak.

But a few seconds later, and against his better judgment, he continued to pump Knudsen with questions about her, avoiding the invite, still hanging heavy in the air. But Knudsen didn't have any other information. It was just some chance encounter at a gourmet supermarket in that beautiful small town. She probably had the regulars drooling red wine on their overalls up there.

With those long legs of hers and the way she could ride a pole in his private fantasies, just like she had a couple of times when they'd gotten sufficiently drunk and crashed a strip joint, she was impossible to forget. That one night she took tips, daring him to steal her off the stage and take her home.

And that's exactly what he did. She giggled and moaned all night long. God, those were the good days. Those were some fantastic days.

"So how come you were—are—up in St Helena?" he said as he desperately tried to clear his head of the visions. It was the only question he had left in his quiver.

"Family's got friends, the Jacksons. One of the grandsons was a buddy of mine in San Diego for a spell. Former Ranger and a good solid guy. They own a vineyard here and a bunch of them over in Sonoma.

I'm picking up a few cases for my niece's wedding."

"Cassie?"

"Indeed. Turned out real pretty. You'd be proud of her."

"Good for her." Derek remembered the toothless and pigtailed niece of Knudsen, daughter to Knudsen's older sister, who was also a major piece of work. They both were after him at one time or another. Cassie wouldn't leave him alone, and she was a teen. Randy like her mother. Little buck-toothed Cassie was like the fly that just wouldn't quit, and he was powerless to stop her like he wanted to because she was a Teammate's niece. Her mom just stood back and watched, weaving her web, in case he got ensnared. He was never interested in her, but she let her intentions be known without subtlety. That seemed to be a family trait.

So apparently the bratty teen had grown up while Knudsen and Derek were off being Boy Scouts. She beat him to the altar, as it were. He had to do a redirect because his mind was getting ugly inside and starting to ooze. "When do you come back down to San Diego?"

"I'm staying over tomorrow and at least through the weekend, maybe a couple of days longer. You miss me? I thought you missed Remington."

"Come on, Knudsen. Get your boot out of my ass. Besides, I didn't tell you the news?"

"What news?"

"Just got the notice last week. They gave me the medical. I'm out."

"No fuckin' way. You gotta be kidding me."

"Swear to God. Swear to St. Frog in a leakin' boat. They did it."

"Don't take our saintly Lord in vain, Derek. This is no laughing matter."

"Tell me about it. You think I'm laughing?"

"Seriously, what are you going to do?"

That was a very good question. It had been the other thing he'd thought about nearly twenty-four-seven. Now that he had the time to spend with Remington, one of her big objections before she'd taken off, he didn't have a job, which meant no money and no stability. And that was putting aside—which was impossible to do—what she'd done.

It was an impulse he knew was a mistake the instant it flashed into his head. Later, he would attribute it to his lower reptilian lily pad pre-mammalian origins harkening back to an early ancestor with no brains but reaction times off the charts.

"If you're sure you'll stay put for a few, I guess I'll come on up there, keep you out of trouble, and hopefully find myself some in the meantime."

He was hoping it wouldn't be just *some* trouble. He was hoping it was going to be a *lot* of trouble.

CHAPTER 2

R EMINGTON BOLT TORE open her chef's jacket as soon as she entered the tiny apartment above the combination ice cream/candy shop, aptly called the Chocolate Coma. Rent in St. Helena was expensive. It rivaled an apartment she'd subleased in New York one summer when she tried her hand at some modeling. Barely 250 square feet, it had a nice view of the street below and sweet smells of fudge, peppermint candy, and strong espresso from that screaming machine. She gazed out her window dozens of times every day, overlooking the busy small town street below. St. Helena reminded her of Mendocino or some of the little towns in Cape Cod.

What was she looking for?

Her ample chest rested against her folded arms as she knelt at the single window as if worshiping at the shrine of her life yet to come, leaning over the sill and watching the tourists travel below. The funny-looking strangers always swaggered like they owned the whole town, with sweaters draped dramatically over their shoulders, in sockless loafers and expensive sunglasses, trying to look like locals. They wore funny straw and canvas hats at odd angles, hiding their eyes and their age. They wouldn't be caught dead wearing such outfits at home. Locals could never afford to look or dress that way. Nor did they want to.

No, Remy thought as she followed an Express Delivery truck barreling below her second story perch, she knew she was looking for only one body—one huge chested man with thighs the size of both hers combined, and arms that could crush her to him so hard she'd be breathless and gladly asphyxiate under the weight of him. He could fill her body with such exquisite pleasure she was rubber for hours afterwards. Only one man could hungrily scan her naked body and make her practically come just watching him examine her. Some men were sexier to look at than to sleep with. Some men were better in bed than they looked. Derek Fuckin' Farley was one of those men—the only man she'd met—who was both awesome to look at and downright dangerous in bed.

He was the whole package. The bee's knees. Every fantasy a healthy red-blooded young woman would ever want, and she'd left it all behind.

Why *had* she left? She let her fingers lace through

her long hair. There was a reason, surely, but she couldn't think, because right now she felt his kiss on her neck as his hands slowly traced down her spine to the cleft between her butt cheeks, squeezing and separating them and—

Oh gosh, it was no use. She thought getting away would help her be rid of him and the memory of that part-physical and part-religious experience they'd shared. But the rubber band kept stretching, threatening to snap her back into his bed, wherever he was. She'd do anything to be there, underneath him, making him sweat as he worked hard to smooth out every sinew and muscle in her body until she was putty and the sheets were soaking wet.

The timer dinged behind her. The bread she'd experimented with this morning while she was at class should now be fully risen and ready for the oven.

She hopped to her feet and dashed to the kitchen counter where the creamy white dough was puckered at the edges in her brand new copper-coated bread pan, the rising form's rounded center smooth and cool to the touch like the flesh of a virgin's bottom. It would fall back down if she played with it any further, so she resisted the temptation to fondle its weight and texture. Into the oven it went.

She looked at herself in the mirror as she padded past the hallway back to her perch at the window sill, barefoot, her blue panties low on her hips, her bra barely keeping up with the good food she'd been sampling these past sixty days while she'd been eating her way here to this quaint little town. Derek had always said she was too skinny. He'd like this change, she thought as she felt how heavy her already enormous breasts felt.

Above the timid din of occasional traffic, the crickets chirped. They'd be doing so all night in the warm Indian summer of the northern California wine country.

Her phone rang. It was Miss Forsythe, one of the CCA's guest chefs who'd attended today's orientation session. A guy in class called her the "Meals on Wheels" lady. Truth was, Chloe Forsythe ran a little string of gourmet food carts that sported long lines all day long. They'd apparently attracted a food critic all the way from New York, they'd been told.

"Oh my God! Miss Forsythe! I'm *so* impressed. You really meant what you said in class today." The guest lecturer had engaged her in conversation during a break and discovered she was new to the town.

"I always do. I know what it's like to come to a new place away from home with everything so lonely and unfamiliar. Your story touched me. I was thinking perhaps you'd like to come out tonight with me and my fiancé, Connor, and meet some of the locals.

Connor has a friend we think you should meet, not that that's on your menu."

"Holy cow. So this isn't about food, then?"

She giggled. "Not in a manner of speaking." She paused. "Okay, I have to confess. Connor saw you coming out of class today, and he wanted me to fix you up with his buddy. I think he can spot a rare vintage a mile off."

They shared a laugh. She was surprised Miss Forsythe's boyfriend even remembered what she looked like. She'd seen him for only a second as she exited the old stone building. "His friend doesn't happen to have a little lady at home wearing a ring or some rug rats does he?"

Miss Forsythe laughed easily. "Of course not. I wouldn't do that to you."

Except that Remy was thinking a night of uncomplicated sex with someone she could not possibly have a future with might be a refreshing change of pace. She'd been used to either Mr. "Intensity-Personified-While-I'm-Grinding-You-All-The-Way-To-China" or Miss "I'm-Going-To-Remain-Celibate," the two characters in her personal novel she was doing dress rehearsals for. She'd give anything to see those two duking it out in a cage-fighting event. Naked.

What's with all the naked images today? This is like the third one. What was going on?

Oh yes! She'd been thinking about Derek. Not really Derek, but Derek's biceps, Derek's thigh muscles, Derek's soft lips that could suck and swallow her tongue and she wouldn't even care. Mr. Derek-Does-It-Hurt-Honey-You're-So-Swollen-Let-Me-Just-Kiss-It-Again-Just-For-A-Second? *That* Derek.

Remy mulled over the idea. *What had been her plans this evening?* she wondered as she bit her lip. *Right!* Watch a romantic movie on the Hallmark Channel and eat the entire loaf of sourdough bread she'd just popped into the oven, slathered, of course, with butter and some fresh strawberry preserves. Dinner and dessert all in one. She could cry her eyes out, go to bed with a comfortable sugar high, and sleep naked until morning.

There it was again. *That makes four times now.*

"Where should I meet you?" Remy finally collected herself to ask. She hoped it wasn't some place where she'd have to dress up and spend a wad of cash. She was being very careful until she could get a job.

"How about the Sweet and LuAnn's Bistro? We can pick you up at say six or six-thirty. Does that work?"

This tickled Remy. "No need. I live over the Chocolate Coma. That's less than a block away."

"Perfect. So we'll see you there about seven-ish?"

"I'll be there. I'll even shower, if you like."

Miss. Forsythe gave a warm chuckle. "Judging by

the look on Connor's face, I don't think his buddy will mind a bit what you come smelling like."

After the two hung up, Remy was happy she'd at least brought her red cowboy boots. Because they took up so much space in her needle-thin closet, it was a considerable investment in real estate she now was pleased she'd made. Her jeans were fitting a little tighter than before, but judging from the way the girls in St. Helena tended to be on the hefty side, more country-style, she figured she'd fit right in. She wore her red silk big shirt, combed out her hair, and tied a red bandana in a bow at the top of her head, keeping her hair back.

With her pale complexion, her red aviator glasses and dark hair, she was looking a little Forties. She applied lots of red lipstick because she was in one of those moods and it filled out her look as well as her breasts filled her double D-Cup bra. She'd have to stay away from the alcohol tonight or that bra might have to go *before* she got home, and that would mean trouble.

Except that's what she needed. Trouble. It was the right kind of medicine, and if this guy was half as good looking as Miss Forsythe's fiancé, it was game on. She was going balls to the wall.

Even if she didn't have any.

THE BISTRO USED to be a hardware or plumbing supply store of some kind, because they had left the old metal bins and racks with unfinished pine floors that creaked underfoot. She thought it charming Country Chic, with mismatched tables and chairs adorned with faded vintage tablecloths. Light Italian opera played in the background as she was greeted by a fresh-faced high school nymph with silky straight honey-brown hair. The hostess' young plump mouth was well-covered in scented lip gloss. She clutched the burgundy, plastic-coated menus to her own ample chest. Remy knew what that was like, being in high school with a chest like a porn star. It took her years to overcome the image of a laminated picture of her boobs—the picture she and her girlfriend dared to exchange by text—passed around so half the football team could jerk off to it in the shower after games. She'd gotten the clear description from one of her drunk dates back then, which had been an unfortunate miscalculation on his tragic road to getting laid.

"I'm here to meet Chloe Forsythe and a couple others. Do you know them?" she asked the young girl.

Her eyes got as huge as hard boiled eggs. "Of course! We love Chloe's desserts and her Greek goodies from her food cart. We buy her things to serve here."

Remy knew the story, just waiting for the girl to get

hold of herself and remember she wasn't there to strike up a conversation with her, but to meet some friends. No matter who they were.

"They're over—"

"Remy! Great to see you." Miss Forsythe hugged her like they were sisters. Though she was a little uncomfortable at the quick display of affection, Remy knew there was something warm and natural about the genius food cart lady. And besides, some of the samples she'd brought into class were seriously world class.

She stepped back after the hug ended, nervously tucking her hair behind her ears.

"And please call me Chloe, okay?"

"Absolutely!" Remy felt her cheeks flush, and she took in a big gulp of air.

"So this is Connor."

Remy shook hands with a handsome, well-built military-looking man, and OMG she knew the type. A little painful, his vice grip revealed fingers permanently bent, one at an odd angle, just like Derek had. His palms were callused from doing the same sorts of things her ex did all the time.

"Nice to meet you Remy," Connor said, being painfully careful not to check out her rack, which Remy appreciated. "And this is my friend—" Connor's palm swept in the direction of their table, where another huge man with shoulders twice as wide and thick as hers was getting up from seated position, his back to her. As he uncoiled himself to reveal his six-foot-something frame, he turned and gave her a grin, exposing teeth too big for his kisser. The man's enormous white pearlies, filed perfectly straight by an overzealous dentist, nearly blinded her. She immediately recognized him.

Simultaneously, Remy and Connor blurted out the gentleman's name.

"Knudsen."

CHAPTER 3

D EREK HAD SPENT the rest of the early morning tossing in bed, without being able to fall deeply asleep. Shooting pain in his right thigh bothered him more than usual. Plus, the visions in his head and the sounds of her apparition moaning in his ear had his body responding as if she were right there next to him. As the early morning light began to filter through a window he'd forgotten to shutter, he tore himself out of bed, showered, and threw some things into a black nylon duty bag. Before zipping it up he hobbled back to his closet, searching the secret compartment under the carpet for weapons, fingering over his choices.

He decided to take his DDM4 300 short barrel, his DDMS .308 long gun, and his Sig Sauer P226. The latter pistol he quickly tucked in the clip holster behind his waistband.

WTF? He stiffened and rubbed his chin with his fingers. Wasn't like he was readying himself for another deployment or special interim mission. But old habits were hard to break. Without firepower, he felt naked.

He made himself a quick protein shake, took his Ample supplements and meal replacement packets for on the road, and left.

With his bag stowed under the seat behind him, he adjusted the music on his phone, attached his wireless necklace and ear bud, and commanded his spotless black Hummer to roar to life like he was doing a victory lap.

The long trip took him nearly ten hours with the sporadic traffic he encountered in population centers near noon and then again at early commute times. At last, he branched off the freeway and headed west to Napa Valley, following the signs to St. Helena just as the sun was getting low.

He was forced to make another pit stop as well as fill up the Hummer, which he did as soon as he got to town, cursing himself for not pulling over at one of the gas stations along the Interstate where gas was nearly fifty cents cheaper. Stepping aside while he waited for the nozzle to shut off, he rang Knudsen.

The phone went right to voicemail. Odd.

With loud music blaring in the background, he could barely hear Knudsen's canned voice, *'You know what to do and how to do it, and, yes, I'm an asshole so save your breath.'*

"Dude," Derek began. "You'll never guess where I am." He paused. "I'm filling my tank just outside your little town, and where the hell are you, bro? 'Cause I'm crashing your party."

He hung up as the hose line clicked. Derek replaced his gas cap and checked his phone again. The screen was still silent, the blurry flesh tones of Remy's backside alluring as his screensaver. He stared at it as if willing her body to come to life for him, which was ridiculous. He jumped when his phone began to buzz.

"Derek, you're timing is incredible, man. Now I believe all those stories."

Derek heard singing in the background, a cabaret or opera tune.

"You having dinner?"

"Oh yea, man. I've got a boner the size of Montana, and it's blocking me up, but I managed to drink a brew and get some breadsticks. We're waiting for pizza."

"We?"

"Yea, some locals I told you about. Nice folks. Family owns that winery, remember?"

"Of course I remember. So dude, where is this place?"

"You're at the Gas-N-Go?"

"Yup."

"So you head straight downtown. Place is on your

right. It has a red awning with a little string of red, white, and green twinkle lights buzzing like flies all over it. Called LuAnn's Bistro. Food smells great. Beer's good. Company is to die for."

"That good?"

"Oh yea. I got you fixed right up, buddy. You're gonna thank me."

"How the hell did you even know I was coming?"

"What kind of a question is that, after all we've been through? You said you'd come, and I believed you. Besides, I think I caught a whiff of you just a second or two ago."

"I need to change? Just came from over ten hours on the freeway, man."

"I'd reapply that deodorant. Maybe shave 'cause knowing you there's stubble, and a nice clean look might impress, if you know what I mean. A clean tee would help, but this isn't fancy here, so if you look nice and smell great, they won't notice what you're wearing."

"They?"

"Like I said, Faraway, I got you all fixed up. You won't believe your eyes and how incredibly lucky you are."

Derek squeezed the phone at being called his Team nickname, *Faraway*. He sucked in his belly until it hurt. "Okay, give me five then. I'll go shave and be right over."

"You do that," Knudsen said just before he hung up.

Derek swung the Hummer into a parking space and rummaged through his duty bag for the shaving kit, retreating to the bathroom for the second time in minutes. He'd just applied his shave cream, so was looking like Frosty the Snowman when someone wanted to get into the men's room.

"In a minute. Shaving. Sorry," he shouted and heard someone curse on the other side of the door. He finished, remembering to apply aftershave and taking careful aim at his part, laying his short hair down as best he could. As he examined his face in the mirror, part of his cowlick shot up like feathers. After it continued to be stubborn, even after applying water a second time, Derek gave up. He searched for evidence he'd cut himself, but was satisfied he'd done a relatively good job. His stomach began to lurch at the prospect of meeting someone new and perhaps being able to peel off the skin of remembrance he still carried. Time to move on. Prove to himself that he could, that he didn't need her.

He gathered his things. He walked into the minimarket and bought an energy drink and some gum. The Indian clerk handled his transaction efficiently. Derek found a folded brochure in a plastic stand for the California Culinary Academy. The headline on the little pamphlet said, *Serving The Community of Veterans Who Served Us All.*

He flipped open the form and found there was a program for returning veterans, which included financial aid. His low chuckle drew a puzzled expression from the attendant.

"Steven fuckin' Seagal. They teach cook school here?"

The smooth-faced youth didn't say a word, blankly staring back at him.

"We're all gonna die," Derek said and allowed himself a good belly laugh this time. He folded the brochure, placing it in his back pocket, and left for the Hummer.

Derek pulled up beside Knudsen's bright yellow Hummer, the entire second seat filled with cases of wine. He was hoping a few bottles would find their way to being opened during the next few days. He guessed Knudsen hadn't arrived until recently since the engine was still warm and no way would he leave nice wine in the second seat of his truck on a warm August night.

He walked through the door and let his eyes adjust to the darkness. He heard a titter of laughter and eyed several people in the corner. On closer inspection, he saw two women sitting with their backs to him, side by side, both in blue jeans. One he didn't recognize, but the perfect heart-shaped ass on the other one got his ears buzzing.

Across the table, Knudsen was grinning like the Cheshire Cat from Alice In Wonderland, beginning to stand.

He watched as the lady's long dark brown curls flipped to the side when her torso turned to take stock of the new arrival. The floppy red bow in her hair matched her bright red shirt. But he focused on her red lips that did not smile. They turned down in a worried look. It was the kind of welcome he expected.

Remy!

What were the odds?

Now the man next to Knudsen stood as well and followed his best friend over to greet Derek, who was still in shock. How could this be happening? He wanted to punch something, someone, find blame anywhere but inside himself. He wanted to run, but didn't dare. And besides, the sight of her with her pained expression was like a flame he was attracted to, just like a pathetic moth.

Knudsen was trying to make light of it, but was having way too much fun.

"—A pleasure to meet you. Knudsen here's told me some wonderful things about you," the other man said.

Knudsen was off-balance and let lapse the big guy's name. It was something like *Conjob,* another nickname for a guy on Team 5. "Thanks, man," he said reflexively, his hand shooting out for the bump. The name still didn't come to him, so he responded with a familiar question, "You Rocket Ranger?"

"Ah, so Knudsen told you about me. Now I'm law enforcement."

"Ah." It was impressive to see someone go beyond their military job description, something Derek hadn't grappled with yet. He was busying his mind, counting lights on the twinkle strand over the table, just so he didn't have to think about or look at Remy. When he finally did sneak a peek, she'd softened. Her face in profile, with her silky red shirt showing shiny parts over her chest and shoulders, only made the situation room between his thighs worse, in spite of his attempt to visualize something dead so he wouldn't have to think about how it made him feel to see her at last. And he'd seen a lot of dead things on his missions, but all he was coming up with was wilted carrots, rotting eggplant, and decapitated potatoes.

Knudsen had blocked his view, so he angled just slightly and discovered she'd turned around and was leaning into the other woman, whispering. That generated the examination by another set of unfamiliar female eyes, and this time, those eyes went from his face, down to his shoes, and back up again, but more slowly on the uptake. The lady swallowed and didn't say a word.

Good.

"Knudsen, this is kinda awkward," Derek finally said.

"Shit, I know. Luck of the draw, man. Not like I was here to tell your life's story, but we were just talking about how we knew each other when you called me. I got up to give us some privacy. But, Derek, bro, I'm glad you're here."

The other fellow crossed his well-developed guns and politely waited, which was smart.

"I'm sorry," Derek said to the man. "I've forgotten your name. Stupid of me."

"Connor. I'm Connor Jackson. Knudsen and I were old friends back in Coronado. We trained together for a mission I'm happy to say was executed flawlessly."

"Got that right," Knudsen said as he slapped Jackson's back. "Come on over and let me introduce you to Chloe, Connor's fiancée. She's a chef. Owns a fleet of food carts."

Derek's brain wasn't functioning well. Did Knudsen just say something about food? It was a foreign thought.

"Knudsen, I need a beer right now. After that, I'll see where I'm at."

"I've got it," Connor said as he left in search of a waiter.

Derek pulled his Team buddy aside, and in a whisper asked, "Seriously, Knudsen, you couldn't have told me about all this?"

"Would you have come?"

"No."

"Well then, it's confirmed. I did the right thing."

Derek was trying to sneak looks at Remy without being obvious.

"Come on over. They're nice people here. Remy looks good. Even you have to admit that."

He'd been less afraid in the middle of a firefight. What was this, that the sight of her made his stomach lurch and parched his throat? A couple of deep breaths and he was able to solve the racing heart problem. He just didn't know what to say to her after all this time.

Like she usually did, she took the edge off and, in that sweet manner she had, left him starving for more.

"Hey, Derek. What a coincidence, right?" Her smile was cool, but he could see by the way her eyes fluttered that she was nervous too. That gave him courage.

"Remy, I didn't even know you were here," he lied.

"Yes, you did. I told you so last night, remember?" Knudsen barked unhelpfully.

Derek gave the death stare Knudsen deserved. His jaw clenched, but he managed to spit out, "I meant to say I didn't expect to see you here tonight. Now that I can see this is a mistake, I'll just take my leave if you don't mind."

He didn't look at her as he turned and began to leave the restaurant, nearly crashing into Connor.

"Whoa! You done already?" Connor handed him a long necked brew. "I didn't get a chance to introduce you to—"

"This is all real nice, Connor," he said, accepting the beer and guzzling half of it down. It helped. Oh man, it helped. "Knudsen, as I'm sure you know if you guys did a tour together, is such an asshole of a practical joker he didn't prepare me for this little reunion. No offense, but I can't be here right now."

Connor casually shrugged and angled his head, winking out of one squinted eye. "I get you. You got a place to stay yet?"

Knudsen joined the party after discussing something in private with the two ladies.

"I'm good. Lots of places I saw back there."

"Yeah, that will cost you three hundred a night. No imposition if you stay with us. We got a guest house we put Knudsen up in. There's another bed, if you're willing." He turned to Knudsen, who nodded.

"Sure."

"And it's nowhere near where Remy lives," Knudsen inserted, his voice barely audible. It echoed Derek's concern perfectly.

Derek rubbed the back of his neck, feeling trapped

but thankful there was a face-saving exit possible. He was looking forward to some rest after the long drive up.

"Sounds like a plan."

"Sure I can't convince you to stick around and at least have something to eat with us?" asked Connor.

"Nah, man. I've been munching on junk food the whole way. Not sure where I'd put it. I think a good night's rest is in the cards for me, if you don't mind." He was starving, but that could be easily solved. Biggest problem was getting away from Remy. Not being prepared for their meeting had him off his game. This wasn't part of his training.

Connor and Knudsen turned to look at the two ladies seated away from earshot and then brought their attention back to Derek. He knew what they were thinking. Why would anybody want to pass up the opportunity to rekindle a friendship with the beautiful Remington Bolt?

Knudsen's face sported the evidence of a bright, but very dumb idea before he could get it out. Derek held his breath and listened.

"Ten minutes. Just until the pizza arrives, Derek. Ten minutes." He held up both palms to illustrate the point. "That's all. Then I'll take you there, and you can crash."

He started to shake his head, but his ego was ramping up. No way was he afraid of her, and that's the way he was looking to these heroes. This wasn't the kind of metal Derek was made out of. Besides, he expressly came up North to prove to himself and to everyone else, namely Remy, he was over her. It was all in the past, and he'd moved on. Cutting and running made him look like he couldn't handle it.

That was not acceptable.

Knudsen's horse teeth and part of his gumline formed a freakish grin. The twinkle in his buddy's eye dared him to the challenge.

"Knudsen, there better not be any more surprises."

"Scout's honor."

He lumbered behind the other two men and pulled up a mismatched chair, sitting at the end of the table so he could stretch his leg out. It also served to give some relief to the boner beginning to return. His errant body part was not cooperating with his brain. The sight of Remy all in red, the smell of her, the color of her cherry-red lips was a punishment too cruel to bear, but he was bound and determined he'd show her that he could.

"Derek, this is my lovely fiancée, Chloe Forsythe," Connor said, as he bent down to kiss the top of her head before he took the opposite end of the table, perpendicular to Remy's seated form.

Her warm eyes greeted him with kindness, and he

found he instantly trusted her. "Welcome to St. Helena, Derek. Is this your first time?"

He glanced at Remy before he could stop himself. He saw her slight blush, the way her soft lashes turned down as her head bowed. No, it certainly hadn't been his first time. Even he had to admit that the lost weekend of play only made him crave her more afterwards. And he remembered every kiss, every touch. The way the feather bed in the big old bedroom felt beneath him as he held her shattering body. He could remember the smell of their sheets, the way her breath felt as she whispered things in his ear, telling him dirty words he had no right thinking about right now. No, it wasn't his first time being here. That had been the first time he'd felt completely drunk in love.

Accepting the honest truth of it, he inhaled and answered Chloe, "I've been here once before." He wanted to say something else like, "I hardly remember it," but that would have been a lie as large as the pizza they'd just delivered. So he told them the truth. "Remy and I were here one weekend." He chanced crossing the divide that loomed between them. "You remember?"

It was a dumb question, but it put her on the defense. Those clear and incredibly honest brown eyes took him in, and surveyed what was going on inside his chest and elsewhere as she answered, "Yes, Derek. Of course I remember."

For a split second, they were the only two people in the restaurant. But the God of Miracles abandoned him, and just as quickly as it appeared, the evidence of what he'd meant to her at one time was gone.

THE SMALL TALK went on for several minutes. He found he could avoid looking at Remy, though she was the most expressive he'd seen her. There was always a bottle of beer or the cheesy tip of a pizza to focus on when she talked. And that seemed to lessen his panic.

The "just ten minutes" turned into an hour, and Derek began to relax. Maybe this could work after all. Maybe there was life without her, even admitting he missed her. Even spending time in the same room with her without saying something stupid.

"I'm going to the head," he announced to the little conclave.

When returning back to the hallway that led to the restaurant, he nearly bumped into Remy. He was careful to make sure he didn't hesitate, to continue with his forward momentum, showing he wasn't fazed by her close proximity. But the hallway was narrow, and as they turned sideways to avoid brushing past a thigh or hip, they were face to face, her warm body in front of him lighting up his insides like she was a candle. The sweet scent she always wore started the buzzing in his ears and made his nose itch.

They smiled at each other like they were sashaying along the dance floor, partnered with other dancers. But Derek felt his smile was nervous, and unless he was totally off his rocker, hers looked strained too.

He had made a nearly clean getaway when she had to go and spoil it.

"Derek, I never got a chance to explain."

She was at his back, so he turned. "Now I would have thought you could have said that sixty days ago, Remy. What's changed?"

"I've been thinking."

He didn't want to hear it, but he was that old moth again, and Remy was definitely the flame. "Knudsen lets me know all the time that could be hazardous to your health. I thought if you had something to say you would have said it."

"Don't you want to know?"

He became Clark Gable. He even angled his head and traced his upper lip with his index finger, like searching for remnants of a thin Hollywood moustache. "Frankly, Scarlet—"

"Stop it, Derek. I'm serious." Traces of anger flared in her eyes. That got him going too.

"I'm as serious as a heart attack, Remy. Back then, yes, I wanted to know. But I'm all over that now. Now, I just don't care."

He saw the lie drill a hole through her heart. Her

eyes watered as she nodded acceptance. He'd done it again. He'd hurt her. Couldn't even spend one free hour with her without hurting her again. He even knew she deserved it, but that made no difference.

"Look, Remy. I'm sure you had your reasons. I tried calling you. You could have returned those calls. Then when I found out you ran off with Ray, well, that kind of told me everything there was to tell."

"I didn't run off with Ray."

"Yes, you did, honey. I got it on good authority."

"Ray helped me."

"I'll just bet he did."

"I went to ask him about you."

"I get it. Wasn't his fault at all. You parade your little ass in front of a guy about to go overseas and perhaps wind up coming home in a box with a flag, and what the hell? Like I said, it wasn't his fault. It was his time. Not mine."

"I didn't sleep with Ray."

"You're trying to convince me he *helped* you, and you didn't feel all grateful or something and spread your legs for him?"

"That's insulting."

"But true, Remy. You see, it's one thing when a girl leaves a man. But when she takes off with his ex-best friend, now that's another thing."

"You don't know how many times I started to write

that letter."

"What letter?"

"The letter I tore up every time I sat down to write it."

"Well, you're right. I got Jack. I got dead air. I got cheery bubbly bullshit phone messages telling me to vomit some sickly sweet poetry. I did that at first, remember? And then you didn't even have the decency to call me back."

"I'm sorry about that."

"Tell it to someone who believes you." Derek was getting fired up. This was way easier than he thought. He tapped into the early thoughts he'd had, before the softening of time. He was wounded. He was trying to recover. He was lost, and Remy left him. Period. End of story.

"I couldn't help you, Derek. It was driving me nuts. Okay, so I didn't do it the right way, but you scared me, Derek. I can't explain it, but you were crazy with the pain, crazy with that look in your eye. The pills you had to take. You know this. You were trying to heal, and everything I did was making it worse. So I left."

He looked at her red boots, saw his hands on them as he'd peeled them off her several times. Her pants were tight, her hips curvier, her shirt moved as she inhaled and exhaled and as she talked. The little red bow on top of her head flopped like red ears on a rabbit. She was a piece of work. And she was right.

He'd been a mess.

Derek was searching for something to say that made sense, but she crossed the space again and sucked all the air out of the room.

"I know you're angry with me. I deserve it. But I just want you to know, I didn't sleep with Ray. I haven't slept with anyone since I left San Diego."

He held up his hand to stop her, but she forged through anyway.

"I don't want to know if you have. Save me from that, because I know we're done." She gulped in a deep breath to continue her speech, like it had been a rehearsed line. "And I think I made the right decision, because look at you. You're healed."

"I limp."

She almost smiled at that one. He knew it was ridiculous too. "But I can tell you're better. You're walking better. Your color's back, and you don't have that wild look in your eyes. You're healthier. I'm glad."

Was she really glad, he wondered as he watched her turn and enter the women's restroom. Did it matter?

In some strange way, it did.

CHAPTER 4

REMY'S GRANDFATHER CAME to visit the next day. She was grateful for the distraction at first.

Harrison Bolt was a bent, dried-fruit version of his former self. He'd maintained a slim physique and had been active in sports most his life, but he loved racing cars. Although not a professional racer, he'd attempted to imitate some moves he'd seen up close in the pits with some of his own in the Central Valley open roads and had nearly been killed in a single-car accident ten years ago.

Though the bones had healed, arthritis had set in, and now nearing eighty, he had to walk with a cane. The head of the cane was shaped with the black gearshift lever from his favorite sponsored car—a Shelby GT. After the death of his third wife and the unsuccessful marriage with his much younger fourth wife, he lived with Remy's parents in their sprawling ranch home overlooking their raisin farm near Clovis,

California.

Remy could see he was in one of his moods. He was legendary for winning an argument and then pissing off the other person so much he'd lose the battle anyway.

"Remy, I'm here to talk sense into you. Your mother's worrying herself to death. You have no money, no job. You should be in school."

"I am in school, Grandpa." Remy registered they didn't know about the tuition down payment she'd withdrawn from the trust set up by her grandmother for school. She didn't need anyone's permission to use the money, now well over a hundred thousand dollars, but her mother would be hurt she hadn't consulted them first.

"Cooking school. You could do that at the J.C., where you could also take some business courses. You could live at home."

Like that was a real option after living with Derek? Could she ever live at home? She sucked in air and fought back. "It's a *great* school. World famous. And yes, we have business courses, too."

"Look, we didn't try to stop you when you moved in with that SEAL fellow."

"Well, I am twenty-three years old."

"But you're a baby."

"No, I'm not."

"Did he hurt you? Because if he did, I'm going to knock the crap out of him."

"Grandpa, you stay away from him."

"So he *is* dangerous then! Those SEALs are wired up so tight you never know when they'll spring. You had no business taking on that kind of risk."

"You're wrong about Derek."

"But you're all alone up here."

"Up here? St. Helena isn't exactly a ghetto. They have upscale restaurants and a police department with not enough to do. The biggest crime in this town is teenage shoplifting and being drunk in public. The trap picking up all the DUIs is funding the new police cruisers and new jail, Grandpa."

"But all you need is one bad apple. You're all alone. You don't know anyone."

She loved that he wanted to be protective of her. But she also knew he didn't expect she'd agree with him. "I can still shoot better than you can. I carry a gun all the time. I know how to handle myself, and I'm learning to live on my own, finding my own way without some guy with knuckles that drag on the sidewalk to protect me."

"Remy, come home. Let me bring you home." His pale blue eyes were piercingly honest. It was hard for her to resist him, but she had to.

"Then you've come up here for nothing, Grandpa.

I'm staying in St. Helena to complete my courses. It's just two years, and I'll have an Associates degree. I can work in any decent restaurant, maybe even travel and work in Europe. I have big plans."

She knew her grandfather had friends in St. Helena he visited, not to mention one or two eligible biddies who liked to organize themed parties for their senior homes. He was the handsome Sir Galahad, riding in on a white mustang the same color as his white hair, driving too fast and making everyone's heart go pitter-pat at the care facility. Though she hadn't been in town long, she'd already received the invites for cookies and tea so the ladies could pump her full of information about her *Silver fox* of a grandpa.

In St. Helena, he got the kind of attention he couldn't get anywhere else without considerable amount of time invested. And that was in short supply for her grandfather. He knew his freedom to go and come as he chose would be ending soon, and he'd be relocated to a similar facility. Her mother told her that while he was sampling the merchandise, he was really looking for an alternative to living at home with the rest of the Bolts. He would love to be nestled in a small town where the weather was nice, the traffic was low, the wine flowed, and the town was chock full of old widows bent on having one last romance before they made the trek to the "white halls" of Silver Acres. That place was where you never returned. Someone started a rumor it was really a zombie academy to rival the culinary school.

So the trip was as much about him as it was about her. But she was flattered he cared.

"Grandpa, we'll have to disagree, I'm afraid. As you can see, I'm doing fine." She laced her arm in the crook of his and helped him outside the ice cream shop where they'd shared dessert.

"You're too young to be on your own."

"I was basically on my own when Derek was on deployment that last time."

"But you had the wives and all his other friends to help in an emergency. Here, you've got nothing."

"But I love it here. Besides, one of your girlfriends would help me out if I needed it."

He scrunched up his face. "Don't count on it."

"Nonsense, Grandpa. Why, the gossip factor alone makes contact with me a rare vintage. They dote on me, Grandpa. Because of you."

"I just never liked the fact that you met him in a shooting range, of all places."

Remy smiled. That had been one perfect day. Lots of firepower on the range where she demonstrated she could handle arms with a big kick, and, oh boy, the firepower later on at his apartment. The man was a heat-seeking missile. He'd been the first lover who rang every bell in her tower. He could hit her target blind-folded. In fact, that sounded rather fun.

"Go see your friends, Grandpa. If you're still here tomorrow, we'll have lunch, okay?"

She watched him unsteadily climb into the low chassis of his 2013 white Shelby Mustang GT 500 Coupe. She could practically hear his knees pop as he collapsed into the driver seat and let out a huge grunt. With the cane tossed to the side, the engine revved. The way he made his exit from Main Street didn't have any resemblance to the way he walked down the sidewalk or got into the car. He was a much younger man behind the wheel of the powerful engine. Most the locals knew to stay off the street when they heard his distinctive rumble. Remy worried for the tourists.

Something caught her eye across the street. There he was, sitting on the back of the bus stop bench, elbows and arms forming a tripod balanced on his knees, chin resting on his hands laced together. He let her take stock of him. His steady gaze was hard to read. But she knew he was inviting her make the first move.

She checked the traffic both directions, and it was only after she was in the middle of the street that he sat up, then adjusted his long legs to standing position. He slid his hands into his rear pockets, leaned back on the heels of his cowboy boots that matched hers, raised his chin, and peered back at her. She saw his chest expand as her eyes swept over the size of him, which was something she never forgot. In days past, she would have placed her palm against his beating heart, and he'd hold it there, toying with the underside of her hand with his thumb.

But that was then. This was now.

"So are you coming for round two?" she asked, regretting it as she pinked instantly. The double meaning loomed between them as it always had. Derek's laugh line at the right side of his mouth twitched as he stifled a smile. Maybe it was a wince. In either case, it didn't matter. Her heart braced for what he'd say.

"I'm giving you a better chance to explain yourself." His voice was gravelly, and damn, yes, very sexy. When he said or did anything expressly for her ears or eyes alone, it always felt sexy. "I wasn't in the frame of mind to see you yesterday."

Remy decided the protection of being out in the open for all to see was better than inviting him in to her place where things could happen if the chemistry was sufficient. And then she'd feel terrible afterward. So she sat down on the brightly painted bus bench, which caused him to do the same.

"You scared me, Derek. You were a different person. I didn't know you all of a sudden. I was afraid if I didn't get out then I'd—"

"Be stuck with me out of obligation."

She adjusted her neck and hoped the new angle would perhaps bring new thoughts she could explain better. "Different than that. I wasn't helping you. I had to come to terms with that fact."

She watched as he looked angry for a split second, until all trace of it left his face.

"Derek, I came to the conclusion if you were ever going to find your way back home, I couldn't be the reason. You had to do it all by yourself. I was afraid of you, Derek."

He nodded his head and glanced the opposite way. "You afraid of me now?"

"The truth?"

"The truth."

"I trust the man I fell in love with. I'm afraid of the man I left. So you tell me, which man is sitting here right now?"

"I'd never hurt you, Remy."

She immediately shook her head. "You see? That's just not good enough. You can't say that. I have to feel I can trust my own instincts, and my instincts told me to get out. You could have done something you couldn't take back—maybe not hurt me physically, no. But you would have said something that forever would leave a scar. You were so angry and bitter. You blamed everyone and everything on your lack of recovery. Eventually, you'd regret saying something awful, and

I'd regret hearing it. You were so full of pain you were totally out of control."

"Well, that's why they gave me the discharge. I guess you were right after all."

"Discharge? You mean you aren't going back to the Teams?"

"I can't. I'm—"

"Disabled."

She saw him wince at that.

"I'd say more *disqualified*. My leg isn't going to be right, ever. It will only get worse the older I get. Like your grandfather. Except I'll be forty and using a cane, not nearly eighty."

"So what are you going to do?"

"I'm working on a couple of things."

"What things?"

"I'm just looking into a couple of things, that's all."

"Can you do private security?"

The traffic began to pick up. She'd already spent too much time out in the hot August sun without a hat. She could see he was becoming annoyed with the conversation.

"Look, Remy. I don't want to talk about that anymore. I'm working on things, and that's all I'm prepared to divulge."

"I get it." She could tell he had one more question for her.

After a long silence, he started in again. "So why Ray?"

He hit a nerve. Remy stood, so Derek did the same, his fingers fidgeting in the denim of his side seams.

She'd asked herself this question over and over again. Knowing she and Ray were just friends, spending the night with Ray, especially while fully clothed, wasn't a risk. She'd already decided to leave Derek when she came over. Already told Ray she wasn't going to be his girlfriend that night nor any night. That was as many bases as she was capable of covering.

Ray listened to her. She told him she thought Derek was better off without her, and Ray agreed. Was he trying to set her up for when he got home? That kiss he gave her as he headed to the plane the next morning wasn't a best friend kiss. But Ray was going off somewhere dangerous. She was proud of him, she convinced herself. She admired him. They parted as friends with possibilities. Not real benefits, just possibilities. Like the dangerous possibility that was standing right in front of her now.

She'd never admitted to herself or to Ray why she chose him, but suddenly, it became crystal clear.

Looking up to Derek, she wanted to tell him the truth. "First, I didn't think I was strong enough to handle what you were going through. I thought I'd mess it up."

"But—"

"Stop it, Derek. Let me finish." She wrung her hands in front of her and sorted for a good choice of words. It was important to say it right. "And because he was the closest thing to you, when I said good-bye to him, I was saying good-bye to you. I *could* say good-bye to him. I *couldn't* say it to you."

"Remy—" He'd reached out to put his hand on her shoulder. She felt herself stiffen and knew she was on thin ice.

Stepping back so that his arm dropped to his side, she whispered softly, "I'm not ready to just jump back into something physical. You can get that anywhere."

She saw him reflexively squeeze his fists. "I'm not looking for that."

"No? Because it would be easy for me to just drop all my standards and forget about everything except the physicality we shared. It was great, Derek. Doubt I'll ever have that again, but that doesn't mean I'm going to do that now."

"So what is it you want?"

She searched his eyes, needing to see what his reaction would be. "Time, Derek. I need more time."

For the second time in twenty-four hours, she turned and left him standing behind. Her head was held high, her neck straight, her heart beating like a kettledrum in her chest. She measured the steps, one at a time, then lost count as she hit the stairs to her apartment above the candy shop. Inserting her key into the lock, she didn't check to see if he was watching her.

In the privacy of her own tiny world, she collapsed onto her bed and cried. She was safe for now. But her heart had paid the price. She wasn't afraid of Derek any longer and what he might do. She was afraid of what she would do.

Or what she might never have again.

CHAPTER 5

SONOFABITCH! HE HADN'T wanted to touch her, reach out to her, show her he still had feelings for her. His plan was to show her he was put back together. That he didn't need her or anybody. That it didn't matter he was no longer a SEAL. His identity wasn't all wrapped up in being a professional Boy Scout. His mission was to show her he wasn't affected by the cards he'd been dealt.

Maybe she'd actually done the right thing by leaving. He barely remembered talking to her those ninety days when he came home from deployment and tried to put his life back together. At first there was the concern he'd lose his leg. Then it was that he wouldn't be able to walk. Then run. One by one, he'd blown up every obstacle with sheer grit and determination, summoning up all the steel he had. He was obsessed with resuming his job on the Teams. He didn't want to be one of the ones who couldn't make it.

The physical therapy was painful, and they warned him against working too hard, trying too hard, forcing himself into a state of mind that was coiled up like a big snake ready to strike. He knew he'd become a nasty son of a gun, but he had only one path ahead of him, and that was to make a full recovery, no matter the pain and no matter how he had to keep crashing through it.

But when he hit that plateau and felt himself falter, begin to reverse course, it scared him. The pain pills began not to work more than about thirty-five percent of the time, so he increased the dosage, going beyond what was recommended. He told himself he was special; he could handle it because of his training.

Then he had trouble sleeping. He knew the sleep deprivation was making him paranoid. And who could blame Remy for spending time with her girlfriends, or away from their home toward the end? Just because he was in pain and miserable didn't mean she had to go through it.

So she'd gotten out before she grew to hate him any more. That's what scared her. Of course she didn't want to go back and revisit that.

Derek watched her tackle the stairway at the side of the commercial shop. He waited to see if she'd sneak a peek out that tiny window upstairs, but it never came. She was a smart girl. A good girl. And it was time to move on. She was way too good for him.

He wondered what would have happened if he'd gotten the letter from Remy that she couldn't bring herself to send. He didn't even ask her what she was going to say, as if hearing it would cement the finality that they would no longer be a couple going forward. She'd made that very clear. His heart was just fine with it, the more he thought about it.

Climbing back into his Hummer, he noticed the application to the Culinary school lying in a light cream yellow folder with burgundy printing. A stenciled block print of a bunch of grapes was the school's logo. He checked the address of the school at the top of the page and put it in his GPS.

"Hold on for the route guidance. You are five minutes from your destination," the sexy voice told him. For the heck of it, he decided to see if SIRI and the sexy broad encrusted in his GPS could communicate.

"Hey, Siri, talk to my GPS Unit, please. Say hello."

"Hello, dear unit. Nice to make your acquaintance."

"Turn right at the next block in two hundred feet," said his GPS, totally unaffected.

"That's a helluva way to talk to SIRI. Hey, SIRI, are you offended? This bitch just ignored you."

"Define Offended. Or is this a joke?"

"Hell yes, it's a joke. You tell me, SIRI. Will I see Remy again while I'm up here?"

"Interesting question, Derek. I don't have enough information."

"Guess."

"What are my choices?"

"Yes or no."

The pause made Derek feel SIRI was actually thinking and weighing her answer.

"No."

For just a nanosecond, Derek let his stomach heave like he'd been punched there by one of his old BUD/S instructors. He turned the corner and began driving down a tree-lined road. A large stone castle-like complex appeared on his right.

"Your destination is one hundred feet on your right."

"Hey, SIRI, will I find what I'm looking for here?"

"Also an interesting question, Derek. Yes."

"Hey, SIRI, thank you."

"You are most welcome, Derek."

He parked around the side, in a parking lot bordered by flowers and a variety of vegetables, like cauliflower and cabbage, used as edible decoration. Two young apprentices in white chef's jackets walked down a gravel pathway with wicker baskets over their arms. They bent and clipped green herbs and flowers, placing the sprigs into the baskets carefully. He knew that even on Saturday the school kitchen was open for business. The tourist trade was an important part of the school's training, or so the brochure said.

He brought the folder with him, at first running up the concrete steps. Feeling the stiffness and minor pain in his thigh, he slowed down to a careful climb. Inside, instrumental music wafted through the hallway. The tall walls were adorned with black-framed pictures of various students posing with what he assumed were world-class chefs from all over. He recognized names of restaurants he'd seen written up in expensive magazines.

An attractive brunette looked up as he entered the doorway to the Admissions Office. She gave him a quick perusal and then a full smile. Her eyes sparked in surprise.

"May I help you?"

"My name's Derek Farley."

She stood up, revealing a healthy cleavage Derek wasn't going to admit he noticed. Her handshake was all business, cool and firm.

"Nice to meet you, Derek Farley. I'm Camilla Bernstein, Associate Admissions Director here. Are you considering joining us?"

He held up the folder. "My buddy told me about your program for returning veterans."

"You are a veteran?"

"Yes, ma'am."

"Have a seat," she efficiently commanded as she

slipped into her chair. "We have a very lucrative package for returning vets. The school can offer you a waiver of fees, low interest loans, and generous pay-back terms."

"Terms? As in terms to pay for the schooling here?"

"Yes, Mr. Farley." She retrieved a folder from the file drawer to her right. "We have a military loan deferment program—" She opened the folder wide and took out a cream-colored piece of paper artfully printed up with the school logo at the top, also in burgundy. "Here we go, Mr. Farley. This is a break-down of what we offer *if you qualify.*"

Derek scooted the chair closer to the edge of the desk, placing his palms against both sides of the notice. It was a list of fees for enrollment. He scanned several options, and as his eyes glanced to the bottom of the paper, he saw in bold a grand total:

Twenty Eight Thousand Six Hundred Dollars.

He swallowed. The number hadn't quite sunk in yet. "This is for the whole program, not the part time one, right?" Knudsen told him there was a guest student, limited enrollment program he might be most suited to. Now he knew why.

"Yes. Not including course fees, lodging or food. This is the cost of the school, *per semester.*"

Derek scowled and darted a hard look at the Associate Admissions Director. "Who in their right mind pays this kind of fee? That's over fifty thousand dollars a year."

"Well, if you'll look on the backside, you'll see that you have over five years to pay it back and, I might add, at no interest expense."

"That's over a hundred grand!"

"Well, assuming, of course, you don't take longer than two years to graduate, Mr. Farley." Her cool eyes were not showing any signs of disturbance. Derek figured she was used to going over these numbers and probably not surprised by his reaction.

"Well, Miss—?"

"Bernstein."

"Miss Bernstein. I don't know a single vet coming out of military service after spending months in the hospital recovering from injuries in the war having that kind of cash. I can't see how any vet like me would even be able to pay any of this back. Do chefs make that kind of money? Because my disability checks would be sorely short."

"Disability?"

"Oh, trust me, I could be a cook."

"A chef."

"Miss Bernstein," he said as he leaned into the desk and winnowed down his squint to show he was serious. "I can cook, believe me."

Her eyes fluttered, and he caught her gulp for air. Then the twinkle returned, and her pallor changed from ice blue to a nice healthy pink blush. All of a sudden, she became a looker, and she most definitely was looking.

She matched his body language, leaning toward him softly. Though very thin, her ample chest got dangerously hampered between her and the edge of the wooden desk. He only took a quick look down at the pillows of flesh all trussed before his eyes.

"I can see that, Mr. Farley."

DEREK BOLTED FROM the double glass doors, racing down the concrete steps to his Hummer, the paperwork for application to the school, including a request for a full scholarship tightly gripped in his right hand. He threw it on the floor and stared at it like it was a dead rattlesnake he'd just killed.

"Son-of-a-bitch," he whispered. He leaned his forehead into his fingers placed at the top of his steering wheel.

He had been just going to walk out and tell the Assistant Director of Admissions what she could do with her hundred-grand school tuition when he glanced at pictures posted on Miss Bernstein's bulletin board behind her. *Class of 2018* in bold, scripted letters was the banner above pictures of a couple dozen fresh-faced students dressed in white jackets. At the end of the first row of students was the smiling picture of Remy.

Miss Bernstein verified Remy was a student in the Pastry Chef course. All kinds of things he could do with flour and butter and fruit preserves passed behind his eyes. He even pictured her trussed naked like a suckling pig, waiting for the serrated edge of his KA-BAR knife blade to release the bonds holding the warm lovely flesh beneath his hands. He would punish her for sending his body into fits of need at the thought of her laying even a single finger on him. He'd kiss her until she submitted, until she was ripe with passion and no longer cared about being bound and naked, helpless in front of him. She'd look at him with those eyes, and he'd—

"Mr. Farley, are you serious about attending CCA or just looking to chase after a girl?" She turned and looked at the name under Remy's photograph. "After—" She tilted her head. "Remington Bolt?" She followed it up with a dazed and crazy smile. "Sounds like a cartoon character, doesn't she?" Miss Bernstein giggled.

Derek fumed, but found himself stopped up.

"Pretty little thing, isn't she?" One of her well-defined and penciled eyebrows rose.

That did it. He'd get even with both of them.

"Give me the forms. You tell me on Monday if I qualify. Because if not, I'm outta here."

In her smugness, she took a long time putting together the paperwork in a folder. "Why don't you think about it a bit, Mr. Farley, and return these on Monday?" She held the sheaf of papers in the attractive cream folder straight out in front of her, nearly out of his reach.

He grabbed the folder, gripped a pen from her desk cup, opened the pages, and began printing hard. She waited all ten minutes while he completed the process, digging into his wallet for his discharge information, his health insurance numbers, and addresses of several former Teammates for references.

When he handed the stack back to Miss Bernstein, she separated the pressure-sensitive forms carefully so as not to rip them and, while doing so, asked, "What branch of the service were you?"

"Navy."

"What did you do there?" she said, her head nodding slightly.

"I blew shit up."

"You made bombs?"

"That too."

As if there was significance to the quality of the paperwork, her slim fingers were careful as she tediously peeled off his copies of the forms and stapled them together, handing them back to Derek.

"I'll try to have your answer as quickly as possible. In all likelihood, it will be middle of next week."

"Nope. Gotta be Monday."

"Mr. Farley, I told you, I'd do the best I can."

"Monday, or it's a no-go."

CHAPTER 6

R EMY INTENDED TO spend her Sunday shopping, reviewing notes from the orientation, and preparing for her first hands-on day at the school Monday. Before showering, she stretched to the sunlight coming in her lone window. She'd been used to a larger place at home and then the small apartment she'd shared with Derek when she moved in. Even that was still bigger than this room. Yet she felt at home here, or was beginning to, anyway.

Touching her toes, she wished she could get some red polish, but had to wait another thirty days before the bank would wire additional funds. Things would be tight. She dared not ask her mother or grandfather for money, as they hadn't discovered the funds she'd used from her trust.

The jobs at the placement bulletin board were all filled by the time she'd called. There was one she didn't want to call at the Wine Country Wet N Wild, an animal park just outside of town. One of the students who saw her mark the number down warned her.

"The owner's a basket case. Usually only guys apply there. He's scary. Kind of weird *end of days* survivalist, if you know what I mean? Fancies himself as a trainer of exotic animals."

"Is this a circus or something?" Remy had asked.

The student whispered, "Trust me. Stay away." She patted her arm and walked off. So it was back to no job, no money, and now the complication of seeing Derek and hoping he'd leave town so she could think straight.

She resumed her stretches, but the consequences of her actions began to weigh on her. She didn't like the feeling she was hiding something from her family, from her mother. At the time, she justified it by thinking she had to do something, had to act to get out of her mental meltdown. The magical, warm sparkly love that had been part of her life and had begun to steer her course was gone. Being perfectly honest, she was grieving. The escape to St. Helena was like a dream come true, at least part of it.

Now that Derek was here, her walls were closing in on her. She was not on her own, because she looked for him everywhere. Even before she actually saw him. Eventually her family was going to find out about the money, and then she'd feel even worse.

Lying back on her mat, staring at the ceiling with

her arms over her head, and watching the lights dance in circles from drops of dew still dripping from the trees in front of the shop, her eyes welled up and she just let them flow.

Remembering her grandfather's comment, she decided to call her mother and confess.

She pulled a cream-colored fuzzy blanket from her bed, wrapping herself in it as she occupied the overstuffed chair in the corner, and dialed.

It was truly June Cleaver who answered the phone. "Hallow!"

"Mom, it's me." She knew her mother was trying to act casual about the call she was worried would never come. But her mother also could read a screen and would recognize it was Remy's phone number. It was a little game she played.

"Oh, Remy! How nice to hear your voice." A question mark dotted the end of her statement—the invisible Purple Elephant in the room pointing to their lack of communication. Remy inhaled and decided not to dance around the subject matter.

"Mom. Are you sitting down?"

"Yes, dear."

Remy visualized her untying the apron she never wore, while Beaver readied himself to tell *his mother* something she wouldn't like, but would be patient to hear. In that world, no one argued. Misunderstandings were opportunities for canned laughter to be piped in so nothing was taken seriously.

"Are you all right? Is everything okay?" June Cleaver wanted to know.

"I'm fine. I'm happy up here. Grandpa's here, and we had a long talk."

"That's nice. So glad you two got together. He didn't call me to say he'd gotten there safely."

Remy knew this to be a lie. Not a big lie, but she decided to save her mother face and went along with it.

"The reason for my call is this. I've done something you should know about, and I'm sorry to have to tell you. Ashamed would be more like it."

The pleasant repartee was gone. She could tell the silence indicated her mother was genuinely worried and holding her breath.

"I took some of the money from Grandma's trust to pay for the tuition here at the CCA."

"What?" The snap was harsh. All the June Cleaver veneer was gone. "How much are we talking about?"

"Five thousand dollars."

"Good Lord! Five thousand?"

"Yes, Mom." Remy knew it was only a small part of the total sum, but most of the trust would be used up by the time she graduated.

"We talked about this, Remy. I mean, it's your money, but you were supposed to tell me when you wanted to use it."

"I know, Mom. And I feel terrible about it."

"Not that I really have any say, but I don't understand why you didn't just come to me. I had no idea you wanted to go to school, especially up there."

"Because I didn't know myself what was going on. And now I feel horrible about it. I really do."

"I want you to come home. I don't want you there all by yourself."

"That's not going to happen. Mom, I've already been on my own. That's the way it's going to stay. I'm asking that you trust me."

"I don't think you've thought this through."

"Stop it, Mom. I'm staying here. Don't do this. I don't need it."

Remy could still feel her mother's resistance, but they ended their conversation, promising to be in touch, and she agreed to contact her grandfather.

She stared at her toes, at the room, at the phone still clutched in her hand, and thought about what she'd just done. She'd stood up to her mother and apologized for her hasty decisions, but in the end, stood by those decisions and asked her mother to trust her. She inhaled deeply and let the breath fall out of her, releasing all the tension.

It's done. I did it.

She scrambled to the shower, ready to start her day

again. Clean. After that, she intended on calling her grandfather.

HARRISON BOLT ARRIVED about an hour later, parking on the sidewalk of the candy shop, nearly decapitating the parking meter. He extricated himself from the speed machine and stared up at the window. Remy knew he didn't want to climb the long stairway to her apartment. She leaned outside.

"I'll be right down Grandpa."

He said something, but was steadying himself on his cane and looking down. Remy grabbed her jacket, slung her purse crosswise over her chest, and slipped on her canvas loafers.

His attempts at smiling were hampered by distraction. It wasn't long before Remy realized he was in quite a bit of pain.

"You okay?"

"None of your concern. I don't want to talk about it, Remy. How are *you*? That phone call I got from your nearly incoherent mother almost gave me a heart attack."

"She told you what I did?"

"Yes, she did. Unfortunately, I think your mother overplays her hand. That money is yours, and I told her so."

Remy was thrilled. "Thanks, Grandpa." She hugged

his arm, and he struggled to keep his balance.

"I'm good. Just give me a minute."

She released him, not sure he wouldn't fall, but he adjusted his hips several times and at last got his balance, clutching his cane for safety.

"Listen, I need to walk this leg out a bit. Would you mind humoring me for a few yards?"

"Grandpa, look, the Bistro is right down the street. Great place for lunch, and—"

"Remy, it's called brunch if it's before eleven. If they serve eggs, I'm good."

"We'll see, Grandpa." She tried to help him again with one arm under his, but he shook her off. "You're as stubborn as I am, Grandpa."

"Apparently. I've heard that before. I can't remember which wife, though." He chuckled, which nearly sent him reeling again. Then he started a coughing spell. After finally clearing what had been in his lungs, he continued. "That's the good and bad of getting old. Half the stuff you don't remember are things you don't want to remember, and half are things you want to remember and don't. In the end, I just take what comes up and try not to get too upset with any of it. Not like I have to remember missile codes or names of heads of state."

"They have staff for that."

"I had wives for that. So you used my Una's money

to begin cooking school?"

"Yes. Chef. I want to be a pastry chef."

"You had every right to that money and always will. But, Remy, why didn't you just ask your mom first?"

"Because I was afraid of what she'd say. I wasn't thinking. I just had to go." She shrugged her shoulders.

Bolt grunted and continued to hobble with the assistance of the cane. "We kind of thought you'd come home when you broke up with that SEAL. We were okay with you traveling. But living up here, all on your own?"

"I'm in a community here." She turned to him. "I would have thought you'd be more concerned about my traveling around California by myself. Now that I'm settled here, I think it's much safer. I'll have a schedule and people who know about me and care." And then she added, "Besides, like I told you earlier, St. Helena isn't exactly a ghetto, and the police have time to write tickets for jaywalking here."

"Good to know." His response was gruff, triggering Remy's concern for the pain he might be experiencing.

"But I'm fine with you spying on me. I kind of like it. We're sort of both outliers here, right? Escaping the crazies of Southern California?"

"Never thought of it that way, but you're right, Remy." He was breathing hard. The walk was taxing him more than Remy expected. "Ah, your mom just had her heart set on you settling down south. She's worried you'll meet someone and put down roots up here." He winked at her and caught her nose with his thumb and first two fingers like he used to do when she was little. "She'll get over it."

In spite of what he'd twice turned down, she grabbed his arm and walked with him, clutching close to him, liking the strength and resolve her Grandpa had always had for her growing up. He was still a giant of a man. Opinionated, just like the rest of the Bolt family, but warm and loving on the inside.

"So what happened with your SEAL, may I ask?"

"He was injured, as you know. Came home and just had so much to deal with. Maybe I should have tried harder, but I just knew I had to let him go." She almost said '*if I ever hoped to get him back, I had to let him go,*' but she held it in.

"I don't blame you. Those guys are intense, but then, I guess you'd have to be to do that line of work. Good for you in realizing you couldn't be part of that. No harm done, then. And no regrets?" He turned to look down on her.

She didn't want to lie to him. "I loved him, Grandpa. But it's getting better."

"Ah, dearie," he said as he swung his arm around her shoulder. "Love is a bitch sometimes, isn't it? You get so close, and then, well, it just disappears. You can't worry about it. But I think you did the right thing. Say what you want about your decision to come up here. You were asserting yourself, just like you did with your SEAL fellow. It's never a bad thing to know where you stand and to take that stand."

But did she, really? After Derek was gone, really gone, and she was in St. Helena all by herself, moving on like she'd always wanted to do, that's when the real battle began.

CHAPTER 7

DEREK AND KNUDSEN sat out on the patio at a German eatery, having a beer and watching the tourists.

"So I guess you'll be going home tomorrow, then?"

Derek shrugged then pulled out his cell phone, revealing the black screen. "No calls yet."

Knudsen gave him one of his legendary horse teeth grins. "Which little lady are you looking to hear from?"

Derek knew what he was saying, but he didn't dare let on. "Miss Bernstein, the Associate Admissions Director."

Knudsen raised his beer stein. "To being a pastry chef. The school will never be the same."

Derek clinked his stein against his friend's just as his cell phone rang.

"Mr. Farley, I have a path to you attending CCA, but it involves working part-time for one of our benefactors. Before he commits, he'd like to meet you."

"Seriously?" Derek's palms were sweating, and he felt himself shake. "I mean, that's great."

"Well, thank me afterwards. Mr. Gerson is somewhat of an acquired taste. He himself is a disabled veteran."

Derek was instantly inflamed. His grip nearly shattered his phone. He ground his teeth so loud even Knudsen heard it and sat up to full attention.

"Discharged. Medically discharged."

"Well, this program is written for a disabled veteran, like Mr. Gerson. And he wants to meet with you. Today."

"Today?"

"Yes, Mr. Farley. I'll text you his address. He's about a half-hour west of town."

"Okay. So he's expecting me?"

"If you want the scholarship, it will require you work for him part-time. But that won't interfere with your studies."

"Why would he do this?"

"Mr. Farley, you're going to have to meet Mr. Gerson and ask him yourself. I'll let him explain everything to you. But he's a former military guy, some secret society. Special something."

"Special Ops?"

"That's it. Super secret. No one knows anything about them, from what I've heard."

"Okay. What exactly did you tell him about me?"

"He asked me what branch of the military you were and I told him Navy, and I also told him that you made bombs."

"Holy shit. What is he expecting?"

"That I can't help you with. He didn't tell me what you'd be doing there, but I would suspect it involves animals."

"*Animals*?

"It's a game preserve. He runs like an exotic zoo."

"I didn't know St. Helena had a zoo."

"Well, that's Mr. Gerson's business. He takes people on safaris. I understand he has beautiful animals."

Knudsen was still listening intently, his brow curled in concern. Mouthing the word *zoo* along with a question mark for an expression.

"Okay." Derek shrugged, and Knudsen returned a look telling him he thought he was crazy.

"Good. Then shall I tell him you're on your way?"

"I guess so. Does this mean I'm in?"

"If you can get along with Mr. Gerson, yes."

Derek stared back at the screen on his phone. "I can't believe it. There's this guy, ex special ops guy, and he runs an exotic game park."

"Yea."

"He wants to meet me today. He might underwrite my tuition here."

Knudsen studied him hard, his mouth forming a thin line. He finally glanced back at his beer and, without looking at him in the eyes, mumbled, "So, Derek, just what does this guy have in mind?"

THEY'D TALKED ABOUT it, argued somewhat, and Knudsen insisted he should come along, since Derek didn't know the area. Derek pointed out that Knudsen was even more a stranger than he was. Plus, unlike Derek, Knudsen also hadn't brought any firearms. Derek was loaded up for a small revolution.

Alone, he followed the winding road out of town when suddenly the pavement ended, turning into a dusty logging-trail-type passage through dense forests of redwoods and tall pines. Several times the GPS lost a map grid entirely, and he heard the sexy female voice utter "recalculating" so many times he finally turned down her volume. This indicated it was a private road and not one maintained by the county.

He saw the first evidence he was on the right trail when he spied a chipped and crooked hand painted sign that read 'Wine Country Wet N Wild.'

The sign had been attached to a fallen and burnt out tree stump, but had gotten loose and the directional arrow pointed down. Since there was no other turnout, Derek continued on the same trail, his Hummer kicking up a small tornado cloud of red dirt.

At last he came to a dense forest and carefully maneuvered around the many charred stumps and massive old trees that showed evidence of fire damage from seasons past. The light was nearly gone from view, the trees were so dense and tall.

Finally, he came upon a tall iron gate resembling the entrance to a small fortress. He'd seen some of these on deployment in Somalia in the outlying areas controlled by warlords. Of course, it was missing the hanging human bodies and severed heads. But something dark and sinister loomed in front of him, and it wasn't welcoming.

He had to exit the Hummer to reach the intercom. A chill went down his spine as he heard a roar from a lion followed by trumpeting from several elephants. It could have easily been a dinosaur from the famous adventure movie.

"Hello?" he spoke into the box. "Anyone there?"

The scratchy answer was not audible.

"Excuse me? This is Derek Farley. I have an appointment to see Mr. Gerson."

Again, static from the box was unintelligible. He walked to the gate then observed the signs advising it was charged with an electrical current; he didn't touch it or try to push it open. From far away, he thought he heard a Jeep motor, but it was drowned out by the sound of a stampede, getting louder by the second.

Out of nowhere, a herd of about ten huge, reddish black long-horned buffalos stormed past the gate. One of them hit the fence beyond, causing a spark that flared nearly a foot. The stumbling buffalo scrambled to his feet and joined the herd as it thundered off. The ground stopped shaking.

He didn't know what he'd expected, but this was not it.

A green Land Rover came into view, painted with a jungle theme and covered with the Wet N Wild logo. Out jumped a burly man nearly Derek's height, but almost a hundred pounds heavier, hair growing from his ears and around his neck with forearms like a thick animal pelt. He resembled a six-foot troll from a children's book, minus the curved lower teeth. As the man came toward him, Derek noticed the large hunting rifle strapped to his back and the KA-BAR kept in place with a thigh strap. He was searching all around him as he traveled the dozen or so steps to the gate entrance. Using a hand-held device, the gate opened inward.

Above the grinding and squeal of the metal hinges, Derek was shouted instructions.

"Leave your Humvee here and come with me, Mr. Farley."

There was no extending of hands for a shake. The nervous Mr. Gerson removed his rifle and with his back to Derek, scanned the brush and trees behind his Land Rover.

Derek did what he was told, stashing his duty bag in the locked compartment under the second seat of his Hummer but keeping his pistol in the clip at his back, the jacket flap covering it. He was glad he'd brought his firearms, but hated to leave his other two behind in the locked case. With his vehicle secured, he entered the compound.

Gerson turned and quickly sized him up. Derek was a couple of inches taller. The man gripped his rifle in his left hand and then extended his right for a shake. "Horace Gerson. I'm the owner of this place."

"Derek Farley. Nice to meet you."

"So you were a SEAL?" Gerson said as the gates noisily closed behind them.

"Yessir. Who told you that, may I ask?"

They heard more thunderous pounding of hooves, which put Gerson on alert. He motioned to the Land Rover and was inside the cab first. Derek looked for a seat belt and found none. Gerson immediately revved the engine and sped off, doing a quick turnaround to the heavily brushed trail he'd come from.

"They run through here all afternoon."

"They? You mean those red buffalo?"

"Cape Buffalo. The most dangerous animal around. I had one get loose one year, and he destroyed three homes about a mile away. Killed three goats, a dog, and plowed through a metal barn without even getting a headache. Deadly, especially when mad."

"I see. What did you do?"

"He got a tranq. Had to hire a fuckin' crane to load him up in my gravel truck and bring him home."

"I'll bet you were a celebrity that week."

Gerson grinned, obviously reminiscing pleasantly on the activity of the past. "You pick your battles here in Wine Country. Not much excitement, I guess. So that was a red letter day."

It was obvious Gerson was an adrenaline junkie, and it reminded him of some of his buds on the Teams.

"They mate year-round, and when they're running, well, they just run is all I can say, and they look for things to crash into."

"Sort of a game," Derek shouted over the sound of the engine.

"I guess you could call it that. Working out their aggressions, I'd say."

"Well, what makes them mad?"

Gerson laughed. "Life."

Derek knew some people like that. He smiled, and Gerson caught it.

"You ever been big game hunting?" Gerson asked and eyed him carefully.

"Nope. I don't have the stomach for it. I've done

enough killing overseas."

Gerson extended his right hand. "I completely agree. I could never do that to these beautiful animals. They were put here on earth by God to remind us how puny we are and how fragile life is."

The two men shook again. Gerson put his callused and scarred paw back on the steering wheel.

"Actually, I lied."

"What?" Derek wasn't sure he'd heard the man right.

"They're hunting, just not with the same finesse you and I would do it. They just run things over as a herd. They don't eat meat. Strictly vegetarians, but man oh man, anyone tells you plant eaters are docile and kind don't know shit about the Cape Buffalo."

"I see."

"I'm going to show you something."

Gerson turned off the trail, winding through a heavily overgrown jungle of foliage Derek was sure wasn't native to California. "You bring all this in here?" he asked, waving to the tall plants and pointing to vines extended overhead.

"Sure did. But this whole area was heavy forest. Thick with brush. Whole place burns off every five hundred years or so. I brought stuff in from Brazil and South Africa, when you could do that. No more of it now. Had no trouble growing them here, and the animals keep down the foliage so there's not much I have to do but keep the clearing free at the campground. We glamp around here."

The Land Rover jerked and came barreling out of the jungle into another clearing. An electric fence with high voltage signs attached was dead ahead of them.

"You said glamp?" Derek asked.

"Glamping. You know, glamour camping. We are in the rough, but not too rough."

"That's a new one."

"Just means we have air conditioning and electric memory foam mattresses in the tents. It gets cold at night here."

Gerson stopped the vehicle. He pointed to the fence. A large brown streak, approximately ten feet long, almost like a snake skin, was embedded in the fence. At one end, Derek noticed the face of a dog-like creature, cat creature. At the other end of the streak, a tail and one hind leg was hung up in the metal, held in place with dried tissue. He wasn't sure what he was looking at.

"This is their pastime. We call this a coyote smear."

Sure as shit, it was the body of a coyote, stretched—more like smeared—over the fence wall by something as big as a steam roller.

"The buffalo did this?"

"Every once in awhile, a local coyote thinks it

might be a good idea to hunt here. They've learned to scramble, even with the electric fence, and get over the top in time, but sometimes they falter, and then they are sure SOL."

"So you never come out here without that," Derek pointed to the man's rifle, which was stowed in a clip between the two front seats.

"You got that right. Yes, my .416 Remington. Wouldn't be caught out here without it."

Derek smiled at the coincidence. "I like Remingtons."

"Well, the ammunition alone for this costs me nearly five hundred dollars for five rounds. I got soft points loaded in first, then the hard tips to finish them off. But it's a small price to save your life if you need it. I hope I never have to shoot one of my animals, but if I have to, that means some human won't get killed."

"Ever been close to having to do that?"

"Only once. But it worked out. Good thing, too, because the rife I had at the time would be like shooting vitamins into them. And if you make a mistake and don't drop him without wounding another one, they'll come back, and it's payback time. They are the most lethal man-killers in all of Africa. They talk about elephants never forgetting? Well, Cape Buffalo are smarter with longer memories."

They headed back to the campground site. Gerson

showed Derek the main house. A bevy of workers were preparing a meal, carrying linens and supplies to various canvas structures sitting on wood frames scattered along the perimeter of the little enclave.

Gerson ran up the rustic wood steps and into a hand-hewn beamed great room two stories high. Off to the left were a pair of offices.

"Come on up, Derek. I got some questions to ask you."

Derek had a dozen or so of his own. Gerson took his place behind a desk with a free-form slab of some burgundy colored wood about three inches thick. A crack nearly a quarter inch wide crossed one third of the top. His desk was littered with papers and a whole pad of sticky notes stuck all over a Thunderbolt connected to his Mac. A couple of key clicks later, a copy of Derek's application appeared, magnified to double the size.

"Navy SEAL, huh?" Gerson swiveled his squeaky wooden desk chair to face him across the massive pile of papers.

"Yessir. How did you know that? I asked you earlier. The Buffalo kinda distracted us."

"I pay attention to the sound of the herd out for a little jaunt to route out any unsuspecting or limping coyote." He raised his leg to show he had a prosthesis going up above his knee. "They planted my real one in

Iraq, 2004."

Derek was relieved it wasn't from an injury with his animals.

"When that uptight little Miss Bernstein—God, I'd love to fuck her senseless, but she's been pretty clear about that."

Derek could only imagine how Gerson would be viewed in Miss Bernstein's eyes. Especially the hair coming out from his shirt collar, probably from his underarms, like moss on a tree in the bayou. Derek thought Gerson was trying to look like some combination of Grizzley Adams and the real life legendary frontiersman, Liver-Eating Phillips, who used to roam around the West nearly two hundred years ago.

"When she told me you'd been in the Navy and blew stuff up—"

"I didn't say stuff."

"Oh, I get you!" Gerson grinned, showing off a gold embedded emblem on his upper right incisor.

Derek leaned forward and noticed it was an anchor.

"I tried to make her say it, because I just knew that's what you'd said. I love making her talk dirty, or trying to. She doesn't like to humor me much."

"Probably thinks she's encouraging you if she does."

"Hell, Derek, she has no idea how it encourages me

the more she gives me the cold shoulder. Still, in a firefight or a war or if terrorists come to St. Helena, she knows I'd come save her little ass any day. I've told her as much a dozen times."

Derek was having a hard time keeping a straight face. This was winding up being the weirdest interview he'd ever had. "I'll bet that goes over really well, Gerson."

Gerson chuckled. "You can call me Horace. Cammy calls me Horrible."

"Cammy?"

"Camilla Bernstein." He dropped his gaze then focused his rheumy eyes on Derek. "I served on SEAL Team 5 in the first Gulf War. There aren't many things I could do with my leg and all that would keep the blood pumping, if you know what I mean. Women are too hard to handle, too much work. But these beasts and the campground, where I get to be the real me and set up my own kingdom, this suits me just fine."

"I get you."

"But I have a hard time finding people who can shoot straight and don't get intimidated with the recoil of a long gun. Sort of means I can't leave here, especially when there are guests or workers here."

"I can see your problem."

"I also will need a cook."

"Well, I'm enrolled in the Pastry Chef module."

Gerson stood, pulled up his pants, and then combed his bushy hair with his fingers. "You help me some ten hours a week here, and I'll make sure you get to be the best Goddamned pastry chef in the western United States, Mr. Farley. And you'll have some stories to tell your grandkids some day."

He grinned, and Derek tried not to stare at the anchor.

"I've already got some stories, Horace. But most of them I never repeat."

The two men looked at each other for a long couple of seconds.

"Well, son, I think we understand each other perfectly well."

CHAPTER 8

REMY WAS READING in the colorful overstuffed chair by her window, basking in the late Sunday sunlight and feeling excited about the start of the new class tomorrow morning. The window was open, and a gentle breeze blew the white filmy curtains back and forth, which distracted her and lulled her mind into a daydream.

Miss Forsythe's fiancé, Connor, told her earlier that Derek had made plans to leave in the morning. She wondered if she'd have a chance to say one more good-bye. Maybe a softer one than the two times she'd turned her back on him yesterday and the day before.

The flesh-toned visions floating about her head had the hair standing up at the back of her neck and made her nipples taught. She scooted sideways, putting her feet on the window sill, extending them through the opening since it didn't have a screen on it. The sun felt good on her soles and on her whole body as she basked in its glory. She leaned her head and neck against the bolstered arm of the chair. She felt like she was floating in a glowing cloud of magic. It was similar to how she'd felt those early days being a part of Derek's life. When everything and anything was possible.

She'd wake up at night and just watch him sleep, feeling so incredibly grateful someone so wonderful had come into her life. His lovemaking was spectacular not because of what he did or because of his awesome power and stamina, but because he wanted her to get the most she could out of their lovemaking. He was totally focused on her pleasure. That's where his came from. It was his mission. She'd never been with a man who was so devoted to making her feel wonderful all over.

Little dark storm clouds gathered at the edges of her eyes, and they began to water as her knowledge he would be leaving began to waft into her thoughts and gray out the sunshine. She willed them aside.

With her book turned upside down on her stomach, she stretched her arms up over her ears, wiggled her toes, and took in several deep breaths, before letting them out.

Just let me bask here for a few minutes longer, she said to herself. She smiled at the reference to Rhett Butler Derek had given her the day before.

"Tomorrow's another day," she whispered to the

open window with her eyes closed.

Something dropped in her lap, and she opened her eyes. She couldn't see where it was, but she was concerned it was a bug or flying beetle of some kind. All of a sudden, another small black object flew through the window.

She looked at the cleft between her legs, and there sat a raisin. A flying raisin!

On her way to getting up, another raisin flew in and hit her in the forehead. She scrambled to her knees to look down at the street, and there he was, with a bag of raisins in one hand and his arm poised over his head, about to toss another one through the window. His shirt had ridden up just enough so she could see the veins that appeared at the tops of his pants, which he always wore low. His arm was packed and corded with muscle. His lips were pursed and eyebrows furrowed like he was really concentrating. And then everything changed when he noticed she was looking down at him.

And he smiled. She was melting like ice cream on the hood of her grandfather's Mustang.

She leaned back and opened her mouth, giving him a target to hit. He lobbed several in the air in rapid succession until he got the goal.

Her heart beat so hard it seemed to shake the floor as she stared down at his huge frame. He took a tentative step toward the curb, then another into the street, still looking up at her. Another step, and suddenly, he sprang into a run.

She could hear his footsteps on the stairs outside as he climbed, in seconds giving a delicate knock on her steel door. It was the call to let him in. Let him into her life again. It was her choice. Her mouth parched, her hands shaking, her stomach doing flip flops, her insides boiling, and her chest in a full on sweat, she made her way over to the door, extended her hand, and turned the knob.

He didn't just rush in and grab her. Derek used to do that a lot. He smiled at her, tilting his head as he adjusted his weight, hips slung at an angle, one foot crossed over the other, leaning against her doorframe. Even after the door was open, he asked permission, like in her vampire books.

That familiar way he looked at her melted all her doubts. He studied every little detail about her, absorbing her spirit, her heart, and everything she had, as she lit up in flames. The images and pictures of their beautiful past, of that perfect life so rudely interrupted by the brave service he gave his country, were the backdrop to the new door opening. It was a door with possibility, and hope for some kind of a future.

"Should I come in, Remy?" he asked.

She nodded her head, trying to remember everything about this moment, because she knew she would want to remember it for the rest of her life.

"You sure?" He gave her a sideways smile as he tilted his head to the side in mock shyness, deliciously teasing her.

She ran to him, pulled him inside and slammed the door behind them.

Their clothes flew to the sides. They got in each other's way, tugging and pulling off her jeans, their shirts, her bra, peeling down his jeans and boxers. She had to help him with his cowboy boots, the jeans, and his stars and stripes boxers that stuck around his ankles. They were both laughing while getting him untangled.

At last, breathless, she was against his fully naked form, her palms smoothing over the hard chest she'd been dreaming about for weeks. She felt kisses under her ear, and under her chin, as he laced his fingers through her hair, brought his thumbs against her lips, looked down on them, and kissed her deeply.

She fell into his body, melting against him, reveling in the scent of his manhood and the feel of his perfectly developed warrior's body against her own.

It wasn't chemistry. His tender kisses told her of his need, and her body responded. Like a dream, all the familiar sounds returned, the feel of his lips on her chest, his hands travelling down to grab her butt cheeks, to pull her flesh into him. She hiked her thighs up around his hips, wrapping her legs behind him. She clung to him as he crawled over the bed, laying her down against the sheets. Pressing her chest to his, she urgently needed him inside her, but he stopped her hands.

"Remy, I was going to say this before I walked inside, and," he chuckled and then gave her nipple a kiss, "I forgot."

She wondered what he possibly could say. "What are you talking about, Derek? You're here. This is where I want you to be."

"I know that, sweetheart. But I want to just say something before—"

She was impatient, but knew it was important to him. "Tell me." She arched her neck and rose to touch his lips with hers. "But tell me quick, please?"

He smiled again as her head hit the pillow. "Okay, so here it is. I've done a lot of thinking, Remy. I've been a fool, stupid, all kinds of everything I shouldn't be. But mostly I've been thinking about myself. Feeling sorry for myself."

"I totally understand, Derek. I've been the same way. Needing to run away. I ran away from the only thing that ever made any sense in my life, the only thing that was pure magic. I almost threw it all away. Never again."

"No. Never again," he repeated. His thumbs pressed against her lips as she opened them. He suddenly rolled off her and to the side.

"What's wrong?"

He was slouched over his feet. Was he crying? What had happened?

"Derek, you're scaring me. Tell me what's going on."

"Just a minute."

He was fiddling with something. When she sat up and came to kneeling position, she saw over his shoulder he was fiddling with his pants that had been left in a heap on the floor.

"Derek, sweetheart, I don't need you to wear a condom. I'm on the pill."

"Really?" he said as he arched up and threw her back against the bed, pinning her with his torso, his thighs under hers, holding her arms above her head with one hand. With his other hand, he brought out a ring and showed it to her.

She wiggled to get loose to look at it, but he shook his head and kept her restrained.

"Not until you give me your answer. See, I had it all planned out. I got a job today. A job I think I'm gonna like. There's this crazy former SEAL who believes in me almost as much as you do, which is kinda dangerous, if you met this guy."

Remy was totally confused.

"He's gonna make it so I can stay here. Stay here with you and become a chef, like you."

"A chef?"

"A *pastry* chef."

She was waiting. There had to be something more.

"So I decided I'd do this with you. I'd do everything with you. No more going away on long deployments. It's just me and you."

"You want my answer?"

"Yes, honey," he said as he let loose of her wrists.

She flung her arms around him, wrapping her legs around his waist.

"Baby," he whispered to her ear as she felt him moving into position. "You wanted time. Well, sweetheart, I'm going to give you all the time you need. You can have every day and every one of my nights. All of my time."

She traced the outline of his lips with her forefinger.

"That's what I was going to ask you if you wanted. If this was going to be enough for you, Remy."

She drew his hand up, clutching the ring in his fingers.

"Yes, Derek. You were always the only thing I wanted. I'll take all your time, I promise. And I'll give you every minute of mine in exchange."

He slipped the ring on her finger. She squinted as it wouldn't fit and only went as far as the first knuckle.

"Sorry, sweetheart." she said, embarrassed. "This is what you get, I think, when you marry a pastry chef. Or at least a pastry chef in training."

He chuckled. "Honey, now you're talkin' my language. I know a lot about training and I think you're just the recruit I've been looking for." He kissed her, beginning the long trail she loved, from her neck, across both breasts, exploring her nipples, to her belly button. "I'd like to design a training program for you that gets you hot and worked up every morning and every night. It's required," he said as he hinted he'd be going lower.

She arched up to receive his kisses. "God, Derek, don't tease me like this. I already said yes."

"I'd like to make it so every cell in your body screams for me, creates all that muscle memory so you get to think about it when I'm not around."

She opened her eyes and peered back at him. "Not around?"

"As in, I have to go to the store, to classes, to work, or get gas for the car. You know, that kind of not being around."

His sexy smile, looking up at her from her belly, was driving her into oblivion. She already had all the muscle memory and knew what it would feel like to be his woman again.

"I can't wait to see what you and I could do with a couple of spatulas and some chocolate filling, perhaps some tasty strawberry preserves."

"Heaven help me, Derek. I've waited so long for this. Please!"

"I think we're gonna cook nice and slow, simmer a bit, take our time, because honey, that's all we got. We got time. And we got love."

There wasn't any training in the world she needed for this. The meal was served, and she was going to enjoy every minute of it. "I'm all yours, Derek. You'll have all my love. Always."

CHAPTER 9

H E SAVORED THE rhythm of their bodies because it allowed him the distraction of thinking about how they moved together without him going over the edge. Today, there was so much more he needed to recall—how her flesh tasted on his tongue, how she flashed him that look when he bit her nipple then turned her chin upward when he took her fully into his mouth. Watching her under the tender care of his pleasure was one of the most beautiful sights he'd ever see. His eyes watered, and he didn't even care if she noticed.

Remy's body had indeed filled out, but just enough to make her softer, stretching her skin smoother, which made it appear more tender. Or that was the way she behaved, anyway. Anywhere he touched, she responded in kind, knowing he loved to see it in her eyes, begging to send her places only he could take her.

He was happy to oblige. He pressed his forefinger down across her sternum and rimmed her belly button before he dipped his head to lap the warm space there and watch her enjoy the warm moistness of his tongue. Every part of her was a miracle. If she'd asked him to say or answer anything, he wouldn't have been able to. It was all Remy all around him, the only thing in the world he'd ever wanted so badly he could easily have died without her. The wisps of hair at the back of her neck called to him as he traced his tongue down, inhaling the scent that was growing stronger—that place between her legs he'd get lost in.

His self-control was waning, and she was encouraging him to plunder her. Her fingernails gripped his shoulder blades then squeezed his butt cheeks, drawing him close to her cavern, pressing him to enter deep inside. He held off as long as he could and then watched the spaciness in her eyes as he gave her exactly what she wanted and more. Deeper.

It was scary how much he needed her, how much he needed her body to begin that slow arousal he could follow, measure for measure, to exhaustion. The forceful pumping gave way to awkward groping and a quick change in positions so he could have her from every side and every angle. He kissed the back of her thigh and bit the crease at her knee while he ground deep and pulled her shoulder down with one arm beneath her so she was tight and flush against him.

Her eyes rolled, and her hands began to flutter,

needing a place to roost. He grabbed her wrists, holding them high above her head and deep into the pillow as he did the same with his hips, sending him against her internal wall and feeling the shudder of delight in response.

He waited for her little moan and the deep inhale before her second one, which blew against his chest and face and signaled she was there. He willed it first and then felt the satisfying release into her while she cried, tears dropping from her cheeks into the bedding. Her legs locked around him, her hands still bound by his strong grip. She arched to press her breasts farther into his. It felt like a kiss.

He kissed her neck, eyes, and her hungry mouth. After releasing her wrists, he kissed her palms, following down her inner forearms to her elbows, first the right and then the left.

Her eyes were still closed as her breathing returned to normal and her fingers traced along his hairline then around and over his lips. Her head rose as she opened to see him, and devoured the kiss he was trying to plant.

His last little releases sent tiny vibrations into her when she whispered, "Derek, don't ever leave me. Don't ever go. Stay right here. Forever."

He couldn't stifle the chuckle. Taking her palm and placing it against his heart, he answered, "I'm right here, Remy. I belong here, with you. Always."

He fingered the ring still attached to her middle joint and placed it snugly on her little finger. She drew her hand up between them so she could see it.

"We'll have to get that fixed," he whispered. "Don't want any doubt created about who you belong to."

"No doubt. I always belonged to you, Derek."

"I know it, sweetheart. But I want this ring stuck on the *right* finger so tight it will never come off."

She liked that and gave him a big smile, wrapping her arms around his chest, squeezing hard. He'd forgotten how nice it was to be loved and needed by someone so deeply. His groin pressed to her hips again, and he rocked her pelvis, his fingers lacing through her hair splayed over the pillow.

"I wanted to get you something nicer. St. Helena doesn't have much selection."

"More artsy things. Necklaces and beads and such. But this one is lovely. Simple, and not overblown. I love it, Derek," she said as she admired the ring again.

"I'll get you something nicer later—"

"And it would be second best because this is the one you picked out for me. This one will always be my favorite."

He liked watching her talk, breathe, feeling the softness of her thighs against his rear and the backs of his legs, the way her breasts undulated when her chest rose and fell. He felt arousal returning and let her know. Her fingers looped around his member as she squeezed and whispered, "Thank you."

He liked that she touched him. Their honest love-making had filled all the vacant caverns of his soul. He was back amongst the living. His days of loneliness in the desert were over at last.

THE LITTLE TOWN of St. Helena was buzzing early because it was the morning of a big tourist weekend.

An hour earlier, it had been more quiet. Derek had awakened to the unfamiliar sound of gentle female breathing at his side and the scent of her hair across his neck and chest. Several of the fingers on his right hand were ensnared in the mahogany locks that caressed him. At first, with the pre-dawn glow approaching, he just listened. Then he slowly opened his eyes and observed her breathing in tandem with his own, watching the ceiling shadows as the liquid amber tree outside her opened window played peek-a-boo with her lace curtains.

As the ceiling went from light gray to cream, and the shadows revealed their outlines more clearly, he took to looking at the patterns and now feeling the bedroom temperature inch up a notch or two. But there was the red-hot flame of her body as it rested against his, her one arm crossing his waist, her fingers barely touching the wet sheets beneath him.

He tried to turn, but felt her stir. He could now see her face in the early morning shine, and he enjoyed the feeling of his arousal, trying to make it approach him more slowly, stretching out the time until he'd be urgent to be inside her again.

He couldn't help but let his palm travel down her right side, his thumb reaching under her to get a quick fondle of her breast as her chest rose and fell into him. He examined his hand traveling down to the back of her waist and then over the luscious mound of her right butt cheek. He let his first two digits crawl over her leg like a spider, but tried not to make it spider-like to scare her, until he saw on her lips the slow smile, indicating she was awake, aware, and equally aroused.

When she turned to her back, his palm was resting on her mound. She bent both her knees, maneuvering him so that he could feel her sex rub against his open hand. Her smile was matched by her sparkling, honest brown eyes and the arch of her spine, her teeth digging into the opulent folds of her lower lip.

He was frozen, appreciating the apparition, yet bringing her soft triangle pleasure. He licked his lips in hunger or thirst, or perhaps both. His forefinger rimmed her opening, and then he dared to look down at the wet sex that beckoned him.

She placed her arms above her head and held onto

the metal bed frame, begging and readying herself for whatever it was he wanted to do to her.

He started by moving to a crouching position, pressing her netherlips to the sides with his thumbs, inhaling, and going down on her, all the while watching for her reaction.

He'd missed these lazy early mornings with Remy. There wasn't any better way to begin the day. Or end the night. Visions flashed through his head as he lapped her channel, making her jump and writhe, of their lost weekend in St. Helena. Like that weekend and those stolen hours where all they had was each other and the excitement of the new universe they were exploring, this encounter allowed him entry into her holy places. Her soul was his. Her heart beat for him. Her thighs needed to be parted and smoothed over in a gentle motion like the taming of a wild animal. Her lips needed suckling as did her red areolas, pert and knotted for him.

He did all that and more as he climbed to her, sliding his arms beneath her, kneeling under her backside and lodging her firmly on his cock.

He held her in place then slid her down the length of him while her eyes watered and begged him for more. He'd wanted to go slower, but at last, he had to thrust into her deep and hard, burying his mouth in her shoulder, giving her a tiny nip.

She undulated on him, against him, over him, drew him into her, and pulled him deep before groaning, leaning back, and then falling into the covers with her knees splayed and her hips raised as he pumped her. The spicy aroma of their lovemaking last night hit his nostrils, inflaming him further.

After several minutes, he'd pumped so furiously he'd forgotten himself and suddenly wondered if he'd hurt her in some way. Her palm suddenly came up against his breastbone in a love slap. She turned her fingers into a claw and, nearly digging into him, whispered, "Fuck me, Derek. Harder."

Afterward, it was all a blur. Their early morning ravenous behavior he couldn't remember, except to ponder that it had been good for him, good for her, and something he never wanted to end. They were, as they'd always been in the past, a perfect match.

So as he lay and listened to the new day in St. Helena, his lungs gasping for air, feeling her wet body against him doing the same, he wanted to say something, but he was so out of breath, he couldn't.

And he couldn't think.

Whatever was to come today didn't matter one bit. The world could blow itself up and he'd die a happy man.

CHAPTER 10

R EMY WAS GIGGLING inside during their trip to the store, watching Derek fondle things with his huge hands and catching cans of tuna and dish soap she began throwing at him. She hit him with a bag of oranges and he nearly dropped everything, raising his voice, "Fuck me, Remy!"

Several shoppers turned abruptly to look at the big man balancing oranges as they began dropping from his arms and bouncing down the aisle like they'd escaped capture. He clutched what remained of the plastic bag close to his chest.

That had her giggling out loud.

"Just you wait. I will get even, you little food vixen," he whispered back as she sauntered close to him. With his arms full, he was unable to grab her like she knew he wanted to. She bent over and retrieved a couple of oranges and knew he'd be staring at the shape of her ass. And he was.

A young woman pushing a cart with a baby in the basket blushed and shook her head. An older couple appeared to be tourists and didn't look on as approvingly. The service boy, Farley, who was a special needs kid, came running up to her.

"That's okay, Miss Remy. I can take care of all of these. You go on shopping."

She gave him a warm smile and noticed his blush. She glanced over her shoulder at Derek, who was still balancing the oranges in the ripped bag, rolling his eyes. He poured the fruit into her cart and helped Farley pick up the rest.

"Thank you, sir," he said to the youth.

Remy turned the corner and started down the next aisle without looking back again.

"You know this isn't going to bode well for you, Remy. You might think I'll forget, but I have a memory like an elephant," he called after her.

She examined his long muscular arms hanging down his sides, his hips rocking with that casual saunter she'd noticed many of the SEALs had, the lopsided grin, the dark stubble on his chin and cheeks, and summed up the vision with a sentence. "That's not all that's like an elephant."

She heard his satisfying, guttural chuckle and then felt him grab her arm as he pulled her into his chest. "I didn't hear you complaining last night or this morning either Missy."

His hands were roaming over her ass and drawing attention as his hips began to move against her. He was completely oblivious to the audience he'd attracted.

She could barely talk His tongue had completely overtaken her mouth. "That's because I couldn't breathe," she said with difficulty.

"I heard you panting, baby," he whispered in her ear. "You're such a big fat liar."

"I'm *not* fat."

"But you're such a liar. You loved every minute of it, sweetheart."

"Everything okay, Miss?"

The voice of the store manager sliced the sexual tension between them. Derek immediately broke from her and wiped his palms on his thighs. He hung his head and knew he looked guilty as hell.

"I'm fine. He's an old friend, and is not from this area. We're just playing."

The manager's face became ashen, his eyes wide.

Derek held up Remy's hand, exposing the ring on her little finger. "I'm her fiancé, but I guess not technically until I get her a proper fitting engagement ring."

The manager's expression was still blank. He suddenly consulted his clipboard and went off in search of something elsewhere.

"You're going to make these people think I'm a real

slut, Derek." She rested her hands on her hips and demanded an answer, adding a playful smile at the end.

"I kinda like that in you, Remy. It's your best feature."

THEY LEFT THE groceries in the cooler bag Remy had in her car, walking the short block to Cloud Nine bakery for a sandwich and something sweet. She was starved since they'd played all through what would have been breakfast time.

The traffic downtown was slower than usual, giving out-of-towners time to peruse the storefronts. Parking places were non-existent at this time of the day on a weekend. They were able to reach the café faster on foot than any car would have.

Derek was fascinated with all the confectionery in the sparkling glass cases. There were fruit pies of every variety, full-sized cakes, and hand-decorated sugar cookies along with old-time favorites like oatmeal bars and snickerdoodles. At the back of the case were individual-sized cakes decorated intricately with frosting that looked like lace. Remy saw he was as impressed as she had been the first time she'd come here.

"These are some of the things we'll be learning at the school. The owner, Mrs. Picard, is one of our instructors."

"No kidding? Can't wait to see Horace's face when I bring some of these things to the park."

They ordered sandwiches on the store's signature crusty, whole wheat bread fresh from the oven, along with a shared slice of berry pie.

"On baking day at the school, it smells just like this," she told him. "You won't believe what they turn out for the tourists and guests who eat at the demonstration kitchen restaurant."

She watched him shovel down his sandwich then finish with a cold glass of milk he finished in just two gulps. She pushed the pie in front of him. "You go ahead. I'll just take a bite or two."

He sat back and rocked the chair, giving her that bedroom wink as he crossed his arms in front of his chest. "There are a few things in life I can wait for. I think I'll just sit here and watch you eat."

She felt her chest and cheeks blush. It was just like the old days. Everything they talked about had some lead-in to a sexual encounter or possibility of one. She felt her lips form a thin upturn in spite of herself, as she strung out the lunch, enjoying making him wait for her.

His cell interrupted his reverie.

"Hey, Knudsen. Sorry I missed your send-off." He gave Remy another wink. "I was kind of tied up."

She could only hear verbal scratches on the other

end of the phone. Through it all, she recognized her name being spoken.

"Stop with your dirty mind. I was a perfect gentlemen."

His smile made her sweat all over. Her last bite of sandwich stuck in her throat.

"We're having lunch at Cloud Nine downtown. Come on by on your way out, then." Derek studied her carefully, his eyes traveling down her chest and over her arms to her fingertips on the tabletop. He reached forward and drew her knuckles to his lips with extreme tenderness. Knudsen's voice squawked into the phone. Derek dropped her hand and sat up.

"Oh for God's sake, I'll buy. But don't make me wait. We have a lot of things to do today." He wiggled his eyebrows up and down. Remy was still panting from the last sentence he'd spewed out. Her blush deepened.

Derek signed off and then announced that Knudsen would be joining them.

"Does he know you're staying behind?" She had to know what he'd told his best friend.

"I think he pretty well figured that out. Last I talked to him yesterday, I was on my way over to see you. We both know what happened after that, Rems." He held her fingers again. "And it doesn't take much imagination to figure out where I was last night since I didn't show up at the Barrel House." He studied her fingertips again. "He did know I got into the school and got a sponsor."

She wanted to discuss their living arrangements without appearing to beg. She knew the chemistry between them was making her drunk with desire not to let him get away again. But Remy also knew that would be a sure-fire way to lose him. She'd not asked what the last sixty days had been like, and she doubted Derek had been a saint. Could there be another girl in the picture, she wondered.

It was time to find out.

"We said a lot of things last night and this morning, Derek. I want to know what it all means."

"Well, generally, when someone says, *'Fuck me harder,'* it means they want the whole enchilada right now and not to hold back."

She threw her napkin at him. "You know what I mean."

"Oh indeed I do. I felt the same way. I was only too happy to oblige."

Storm clouds began to form in the back of her head, and that little monster fear, perhaps a little jealousy, slid their way from the back to the front. The smart move would be not to say anything. But she wasn't being smart today. She'd accepted a ring from him, on impulse, not knowing really what she was getting herself into again, just like the first time she'd fallen for him. Had she been foolish? Was this a critical error and could she trust her own judgment?"

"Can I ask a question?"

"Go right ahead."

"Is there anyone else?"

"No." Derek wrinkled his face up like a prune. "How could there be? Look, Remy, I bought that ring. Besides, it's only been sixty days—"

"We broke up a few months before that, Derek. You weren't 'there' at all. I want to ask just because it's needling me to death. Did you meet anyone else during that time?"

She was regretting the words before they left her mouth. Derek wasn't liking the line of questioning. She didn't blame him one bit.

"I asked you to marry me, Remy. Doesn't that count for anything?"

She knew she was on dangerous ground. "It does. But I still want to know. I want the truth, Derek. I heard the rumors. I want to know what happened."

He tried to take another bite of the pie, but just put the fork down, and sighed. Now she was afraid of the answer he was going to give.

"You're gonna think I'm pretty stupid."

This surprised her. "Go on."

"I tried to—maybe two, three times. I tried to get

drunk enough so that I'd think I was with you."

He winced, readjusted his torso, and leaned onto the table. His blue eyes tugged at her heart, and she decided to accept whatever he was going to tell her and never ask again. She held her breath.

"Ladies don't like to be called other ladies' names."

Her chest was fluttered, hyperventilating, hoping, and waiting.

"All I saw was *you*. It was *always* you. You ruined me for anyone else, Remy. I just accepted the fact that no matter how many years it took, I'd compare every-one I'd ever meet to you—the one who got away."

She let the delicious comment settle on her like warm snowflakes she could bask in and remember her whole life. She didn't want to rush her response.

"Who *almost* got away, Derek. But you found me."

He reached for her hand, and she gave it to him. "Yes, I did. I certainly did." He gave her another sexy smile full of possibilities. "Thank God for Knudsen's call. I know all this is so fast, but dammit, I don't want to lose you again. We knew each other pretty well before my accident. The guy you had to put up with at the end wasn't me." He put her palm against his heart. "This is the real me. No one else has ever occupied this space."

It was such a romantic gesture she could have pounced on him right there in the little bakery, and she was suddenly relieved and grateful she'd brought it up.

"Thank you. I love you, Derek. I always have." She felt the tears spill over and down her cheeks.

"Holy crap!" The booming voice of Knudsen crashed through the shop, making every customer seated or ordering take notice. "You guys just ruined my day. Now I gotta drive back ten hours and think of you two love birds doing God knows what. And here I am, all alone." He loomed over their table.

"So the King of Good Times is back," Derek barked. "Sorry, man, ain't my fault you're alone, you dumb frog. But just because you're miserable, why do I have to be? Don't you forget, you're the one who told me where to find her. All your fault, my man."

She had to chuckle at this, which didn't go over well with Knudsen.

Derek's big-mouthed friend looked around at the spectacle he'd caused in the little bakery. Both of them were *way* out of their element, she thought, and Knudsen was not adjusting well.

"So, Faraway, before I say something I'll regret further, I'm supposed to personally invite you to Cassie's wedding. And now she wants you in the wedding party, you asshole."

Knudsen whispered the A word but it still carried. Remy was getting uncomfortable with his lack of restraint.

Derek dropped Remy's hand and stood, giving Knudsen a soft punch to his shoulder. "You watch your language Horseteeth. Besides, I can't do that. I've got school."

"Nah, nah, don't do that. I already checked. You have a break in early October. I had this conversation with Cassie. She's got you hog-tied, man. No way you can get out of this one."

"Except that's a long way back down there, and I'm trying—"

"Don't do that, Derek. You made it in a few hours, *and* you're being a pussy. Just because you're out of the Teams doesn't mean you're out of the community. You know you have to be there." He looked down to address Remy. "The kid idolized Derek. Wouldn't leave him alone when she was what, thirteen? Fourteen?" He straightened up and gave Derek a smirk as if to say, *try to get out of that one.* He proudly crossed his arms over his chest and leaned back on his heels.

Derek was growling, a long frown taking up most of his face. He slowly shook his head.

"We'll both go," Remy blurted out, hoping she'd said the right thing. "I have lots of friends there, too, remember?" She placed her hand on his thigh, the engagement ring glistening in the sunlight. This was not lost on Knudsen. "It will be okay. We can announce our engagement. It's just a wedding, Derek.

What can happen at a wedding?"

"You gotta do this for Cassie, for my sister, for all of us, man. You don't get to escape that easily, or they'll come up here and drag your ass back down there. You know they will."

"She making you wear dress whites?"

"Nope, which is good for you. But she wants an all-SEAL contingent."

"*Former* SEAL."

"I stand corrected. So I can tell her you're in?"

"I still don't want to, no offense."

"It'll be good to see everyone again. You *know* it will."

"Fuck you. So tell me this. How would the groom allow all these frogs to share the stage with him?" asked Derek.

"He's a newbie on Kyle's SEAL Team 3. Wants to get hitched before he deploys. You kinda know the family." Knudsen's worried look spilled over to Remy.

"Who is he?" Derek whispered cautiously. She noted a slight wrinkle of fear present.

"You know him. Ray's little brother, Pete. You must have met him."

Derek fisted his hands. Remy remembered the younger brother, who had been going through BUD/S when Ray deployed. Now she was rethinking the whole scenario, because no doubt Ray would be back from deployment by October.

"You didn't have the balls to tell me that first?" Derek said with extreme restraint. The veins at the sides of his neck popped out and everything from his chin down was bright red.

"And you would have embarrassed yourself by saying no. Cassie didn't know where you'd taken off to until I spoke with her this morning. Tag, you're it, Derek. Face the music. And I think it will be good for both of you."

Remy reacted, stood, and was going to say something about who he was to think he knew what was good or bad for her? She resented his liberty with her future plans. But that's the way the Teams were. You married into them. You were a part of them. The good with the bad. Derek grabbed her hand, calming her.

"Okay. Have it your way," he finally said. "Now, what can I get you? And you're gonna get it to go, because I want you to leave Remy and I alone, now that you got what you wanted." Derek motioned for her to sit and began walking to the counter.

Knudsen followed behind him, wagging his tongue and not being careful at all. "What I want is someone to look at me like she just looked at you when I walked in," Knudsen responded, turning around to wink at Remy.

Again, too many liberties. Too familiar. She wanted

Derek all to herself. A private life. But now she understood that would never be. He'd been a SEAL, a highly decorated one at that. And he'd always be that until the day he died. All her former fears came rolling back to giggle like puppets on a string. What was she thinking?

"So that will be an egg salad on whole wheat, then?" Derek answered calmly.

"Exactly."

CHAPTER 11

DEREK BEGAN ORIENTATION the next day. His move-in to Remy's apartment was simple. He brought in his duffel bag, leaving his firepower locked in the secret compartment under the floorboards in the front seat of his Hummer. All he had was enough clothes to last three days, so everything had to be washed. He needed to wear a clean shirt and pair of pants to his first day.

Remy had returned to her class schedule, and he waved as their group of fifteen new students toured the buildings and wound up in the kitchen, where she was working. Her white jacket was rolled up nearly six inches at the wrists. Her hands and fingers were immersed in flour as she watched the pastry chef instructor demonstrate how to make basket-weave and other cutout patterns in crust for fruit pies.

Several of her classmates noted his wave and whispered together in a private huddle.

Later, the new pastry recruits were shown their

storage lockers, and issued two white jackets with their names embroidered on it. He stood for a class picture, and then a private headshot. It was the first time he'd donned the white jacket. He felt like Steven Seagal.

Due to lack of sleep, he dozed off several times while the standards of behavior were monotonously read over by Alexi Ping, their class advisor, and Asian Cuisine instructor. Derek pondered about the wisdom of having someone not specializing in pastry being their class monitor, and wondered if perhaps this was an entry level job for Ping. He noted the diminutive chef seemed to relish telling them what they could *not* do, several times making cool eye contact with him. Derek had known men like that on the battlefield and quietly decided to be on alert for a blindside. Rarely in tough battles, these regulars sent you into harm's way from the comfort of a concrete bunker with air conditioning or office in Norfolk.

He hoped Ping didn't have that Sixth sense Derek had, assessing men quickly and internally being on guard. He willed himself to relax, deciding his nerves were making him imagine enemies at a culinary school, for Chrissakes! It was unknown territory for him, but it shouldn't be dangerous.

He shook himself, trying to focus, but then all he could visualize was the shape of Remy's backside, and the dimples adorning the smooth flesh atop her butt cheeks—and that perfect ass. The fantasies of her, loving her, watching her ecstasy, were distracting him. It took a minute to discover that the teacher was talking to him personally. The class waited until Derek came to.

"I'm sorry. I've not been sleeping well. What did you ask me?" He knew better than to be caught off guard by this man. He'd worked to make his tone and voice inflection neutral.

"I asked for a show of hands who had worked in a commercial restaurant, Mr. Farley, and if anyone had *baking* experience," Ping added abruptly.

"No, sir. But I can make a mean goat stew or spit-roasted rabbit."

A couple of the students laughed until they realized he wasn't kidding. Someone whispered, "Oh my God."

"And where did you learn to roast rabbit and make goat stew?" the instructor asked.

"In the military, sir. On deployments, especially in away outposts."

The instructor was not amused. Narrowing his eyes, he looked up to Derek, who was easily a foot and a half taller than the chef. His left eye twitched and his hands balled into fists. "I will endeavor to remember those details, Chef Farley. I have to add, I'm not sure— the CCA's pastry chef program doesn't seem like a very good fit for you."

He took a long, hard look at Ping and noticed he had muscles of steel in his forearms, his shoulders were large for his small size, and he walked with a dancer's gait, a sure sign he'd had extensive martial arts training.

"Duly noted, sir. I'm here to prove that theory wrong."

It was a standoff.

Get a grip, Farley. You're doing this to broaden your horizons and create a vision of new life with Remy. Your fighting days are over.

Or were they? He had water buffalo to wrestle, pancakes to cook for hungry campers and tourists who thought they were daring the wild to come hang out at the zoo. But he also had a wedding to go to, and something told him it would be a complete disaster.

MIMI LEMIEUX WAS the assistant pastry chef-instructor and was teaching their introductory class. Her cute little French accent was charming. She'd braided violas into the tiny buns atop her head that made her look more like a pert little alien with antennae. She was skinny—too skinny. And her long lashes brushed over cheekbones the color of the light pink lip gloss she wore.

He was enchanted by the little waif, staring too long and eventually picking up her attention.

"Is there something wrong, Mr. Farley?" she said, raising her eyebrows and waiting for a logical explanation.

How could he tell her he just liked to watch her move, do anything. He could listen to her read an encyclopedia.

He cleared his throat, or he'd have sounded like a teenager. "No." Then he thought better of his answer. "I was just trying to figure out your accent. You're from Belgium?" He knew it was the wrong answer, but he'd learned it was wise to err on that side than mistake her the other way around.

"Oh, very good! You are a student of languages, then?" Her face lit up like evening at one of the mosques he'd waited outside all night over in the sandbox. Derek was shocked he'd gotten it right, in spite of his efforts to do it wrong.

"Just a lucky guess." He tried to shrug it off, but the little chef wouldn't have anything of it.

"You see, class, you must pay attention to detail all the time. When you are presenting your desserts to your public, you might be serving someone of royalty or a very famous person or captain of industry, and never know it. You can't tell who people really are. You present your food, and you show it proudly, with confidence and delicacy."

Derek was drooling.

"Mr. Farley, you come over here and help me with this demonstration."

He was feeling very large and very clumsy next to the petite instructor who smelled as great as she looked. He was ashamed to realize his body began to react to the pheromones she was giving off. It was destroying his heart and making his thinking fuzzy.

"Right here. Stand next to me and do everything I do," she said.

He lumbered around the counter to face the students of his class. It was the first time he noticed several of the girls were definitely giving him the come-on. One of the men looked to be nearly bursting a gut, while another one had no expression at all, appearing not to take notice of anything but the demonstration table. Derek took up position and placed his hands on the white Corian countertop.

"You must be precise with your measurements, class. Like this." She picked up a metal measuring cup, scooped up flour, and leveled the top with a knife. "Mr. Farley, you do the same."

He obeyed, his hand shaking, and shaking even more when Miss Lemieux leaned into his arm, but also touched his thigh, which didn't help Derek's concentration one bit. She handed him her knife, placing her hand over his as she steadied him, and together, they wiped the excess off the top of the measuring cup.

"Voila!" She exclaimed. "Now, I've seen some chefs tap the cup to make the flour behave." She turned to look into Derek's eyes and batted her silky long eyelashes. The sparkle of a sweet soul came through loud and clear. There was no agenda or baggage there. No resentment, fear, or distrust. Just like a little bird in the palm of his hand, he was careful not to jerk or speak too loud or even breathe hard.

"What would that do?" she asked him innocently, fluttering those long black lashes. Her pink lip gloss enhanced the little donut she made of her lips.

"Excuse me?" Derek's voice broke, and the class giggled. Their faces were not more than six inches apart.

"If I tapped the cup instead of scraping the top, what would that do? Think, Mr. Farley. I'm sure you know the answer."

The answer was that Derek all of a sudden wanted to be anywhere but here in this room with all these young eyes on him. They didn't know what he used to do, how he lived, and how damaged he was inside sometimes. He wanted to fit in, but he didn't.

And, as if that wasn't enough, he picked up something out of the corner of his eye. Remy's face appeared in the window of the classroom door.

And she wasn't smiling.

CHAPTER 12

"REMY, I WASN'T flirting!"

"Oh really, Derek? You don't think I can recognize an obvious 'come fuck me'?"

"She's just a child, Remy. Barely old enough to drive, I think. You can't be serious."

"Spare me the defense, Derek. It used to happen down in San Diego. I got so used to sharing you with everyone down there, I halfway wondered if I had any claim on you myself."

All the former questions and hurts she'd lived with, though Derek had sworn he'd been faithful, came rushing back. She'd forgotten about that. The reason for the breakup had been his painkillers and mood. But the attention he always got from the ladies, especially the beautiful ladies in San Diego, was a close second.

She never liked how the other SEAL wives and girlfriends found it necessary to put their hands on his chest, or ask him to dance in suggestive ways. Remy swore she wasn't that kind of girl, and never wanted to be. It was all entertainment, and the other SEALs loved it. But she did not. And she knew many of the SEAL wives didn't, either.

She didn't want to be a statistic or one of those rumors that proved true. And she didn't want to worry about his fidelity, either. That was never going to work for her. She wanted him to go out of his way to prove it, too.

"Remy," Derek whispered as he set down his books and reached out.

She stepped back, not allowing his touch. But he bridged the gap in one long step and grabbed her. "There is only one woman on my radar. Sure, I look. We all look, honey. I'll bet you do too."

She pulled away, disagreeing with his comment. "Here, Derek? Have you seen the guys here? It's mostly women—young, attractive women in this school."

"So you want me to change my course trajectory? I did it so we could work together."

He threw his arms around her, and although she struggled, he wouldn't let her leave. It was exactly what she needed. Reassurance. And she also knew she couldn't always depend on that happening and would have to watch this need or she'd push him away.

Remy allowed herself to melt into his chest. "I like the way we work together. I just don't like seeing you work—so closely—with someone else."

He kissed the top of her head and fingered her hair behind her ear, whispering, "Nobody will ever be as close as you are, sweetheart. I want nothing more than to work side by side with you. I wish we could work naked then go have sex and go back to making pies and cakes and then get all hot and bothered and lick chocolate sauce off each other's bodies. That's why I'm here. How about you?"

She couldn't help but giggle.

"So you're saying you're not a serious chef?"

"Oh man," he said, grinding his hips against hers. "I'm so fuckin' serious, so serious about doing all that and more. I want to play, have fun, make lots of wet sticky love, and fuck you hard all night long so you think about it all day the next day and maybe the next. Remember, you're cooking with a SEAL, baby."

She was grateful for his humor and his willingness to make her feel comfortable. She'd asked for this twice now.

Remy knew it wasn't going to be a good idea to keep pushing for that payoff. She vowed to get herself toughened. Besides, she was going to be spending the rest of her life with any woman's fantasy man. Most women wouldn't be so lucky as to even meet someone so handsome, strong, and wonderfully sensitive inside. And Derek was going to put his tent up over her, and all she wanted to do, no matter where they lived, was to be his woman. But to match him, strength for strength, she'd also have to harden herself up to the realities of a world full of lonely women.

And somehow make it okay when they fell in love with her husband, even if it was from afar.

THEY ATTENDED A mandatory session in the auditorium. Several of the faculty were seated on the dais, and to the side was a gentleman Remy had seen somewhere before. He was speaking to two men, one holding a camera. She watched as the gentleman in the suit scanned the crowd and then pointed her out, which got her feeling self-conscious, and she blushed, giving them a glowing smile.

The suited gentleman came to the microphone and introduced himself as John McCormick, one of the celebrity chefs—and a pastry chef at that—who had a television program on cable. She'd watched his demonstrations avidly before she came up to St. Helena. It was rumored he had a small financial stake in the school.

"Ladies and gentlemen, we have some great news. As you know, my cooking show has just been picked up for another season, and—"

The room erupted in applause. Derek leaned into her.

"You ever heard of this guy?"

"Of course. He's got a great following. I used to

watch it all the time when you were overseas."

"Hmmm. Guess I'll have to pay more attention, then, since he was in my house when I was away," he whispered.

Two girls in front of them turned and put their fingers to their lips. "Shhhh," one of them said, softly.

McCormick grinned, basking in the applause. "So we also have some other exciting news. The Cooking Network has approached us about doing a series for them, called "Life at the CCA"."

The audience was loudly approving.

"I've got some great ideas for some of these shows, and it will be sort of a cross between a reality show and a cooking elimination, except the only people who get to vote will be the audience."

He gave Derek a nod. "I'm going to base the first couple of shows on our male members of the class here at Pastry 101. Not many of you know that we sort of have a celeb in our midst."

He pointed to Derek with his full palm. Derek looked all around him, uncomfortable with the attention, especially since the lights on the camera had come on. Remy could feel the heat as the cameraman ran towards them.

"I didn't sign on to this," Derek whispered.

"Just go with it. I'm sure it will be harmless."

"I'm a low profile guy. I don't—"

But McCormick was stepping carefully down the aisle and then shoving his microphone into Derek's face. Her big former SEAL just sat there, waiting for instructions.

"Say something, Derek," she whispered to him. McCormick was breathing hard from his little run up the auditorium stairs.

"Hello?"

Derek said it like he was testing for sound. The mostly-female audience burst out in a mixture of laughter and applause.

"So this is Derek, everyone," McCormick said to the audience. "Tell them, Derek, what you used to do before coming to cooking school."

"I—I was in the military."

"What branch?"

"The Navy."

"So were you one of those guys who works on submarines or swabs the ships?"

"I was on some submarines, and I did my share of washing things down, yes."

The ladies started to giggle. Remy was getting annoyed with McCormick and the spectacle he was making of her fiancé.

"But weren't you part of an elite group?" McCormick insisted.

Derek glanced from one side of the room to the other, inhaled, and then spit out the words. "I was on a SEAL Team."

It was as if they were at a rock concert the way the women screamed when they heard the words.

Remy's overwhelming instinct was to save Derek from all this, but before she could spring into action, McCormick was leading him down the aisle and up onto the stage. Derek's hands were tucked into the pockets of his only pair of long pants. His white shirt was clean, but wrinkled. His red tie was crooked and hanging more on one side due to the heat of the day. There was no way Derek's physique could hide from the consuming eyes nor could he hide the fact that he was embarrassed as all hell, which only made the clapping and audience eruption worse. People were clicking their cells. Remy was worried about the protocol of having his face splashed over the internet as his picture was being shared.

At last, their eyes connected. That's when she realized how much pain he was in. It was one thing to sign up for a chance at a new life with her as a pastry chef. It was quite another to be dangled in front of some adoring females like the dessert he truly was.

She gave him a soft smile, hoping he could see she understood how he was feeling, and decided to make sure to acknowledge what a big step he was taking. And that he was taking it for her.

She couldn't think of any other time in their relationship that she'd loved him more.

My forever man.

CHAPTER 13

DEREK TOOK A long shower alone. Remy must have sensed she needed to give him space, because she didn't join him. Her stall was so tiny, it would be impossible not to be thigh to thigh or chest to chest against her, and he really wanted to think.

Water always was good for thinking. He'd gotten used to doing it during his endless hours of training, mostly to get his mind off the boredom of pushing for so many days so hard. He kept telling himself the speed was important during those long training days, but it was the *not quitting* that made or broke a young man.

He'd been looking for a steady rhythm of life without the peaks and valleys he'd experienced before with Remy when he was on the Teams. Being here and reconnecting with her had been a dream for him, something he'd pondered every night before he went to bed. He wondered what she was doing, and if she was happy. He hadn't been sure, if he ever saw her again, it would turn out the way it did, but now he was doubting himself.

Derek hadn't signed on to become the school mascot or a spectacle. These people were being idiots. Remy wasn't pushing, which was smart. After all, it wasn't her job to defend him, which would have been even more mortifying. He was grateful there. But he didn't like being dangled like eye candy in front of women he didn't care a flip about. He felt like a piece of meat or a stripper on a pole somewhere. It looked like he couldn't just come into town, hook up with Remy, and have a nice uneventful life. This afternoon had changed *everything*. The second-guessing would continue until he figured it all out and got settled. But he had to wait for that to happen first.

"Dammit," he whispered under the water.

So maybe he couldn't handle this kind of baggage. Or maybe he was fooling himself. Being the adrenaline junkie he was, perhaps it was folly to think he could find happiness without it. But he didn't want to be a pet lion with a gilded cage, and that's how he was beginning to feel. The attention he was getting was more painful than being alone and ignored. He wondered if he shouldn't have stayed that way. He could have dealt with the pain and loneliness. He was built for that. Perhaps they'd rushed into things too soon.

He felt hot tears well up and get washed away by

the water spray.

They didn't know that he'd seen children hacked to death and women's skulls ripped apart by a .38 round to the back of the head. He'd had to kill boys not more than two or three years younger than the average age of this crowd in school. He'd lived by moonlight, sleeping during the day, and keeping himself warm with his own urine. The only thing sweet in that universe was being able to get ten minutes of uninterrupted rest. That was as sweet as sugar to him and gave him energy to last another twenty-four hours hiding in a cave or buried under a truck in sand, waiting for the order to go.

He'd even learned to enjoy the taste of goat, though everyone lied when they told him it tasted just like chicken. He'd seen so much bloodshed that he was considering becoming a vegetarian. Dressing up a roast looked too much like dressing a corpse for burial.

So this was the biggest risk of it all, being haunted by these thoughts of surviving, not being able to go back and experience that deep something—that intensity of being saved by someone, that someone had his back and would give their life for him if necessary, because that's how they all trained. He also knew that nothing else in the world would be anything like serving on his SEAL Team, and living in that Brother-hood of SEALs. He liked being the one to carry the weight, get it done. It was impossible for anyone else to understand, no matter how much they cared about him.

He wondered how God did it, hearing man's problems, listening to the whining and bitching and seeing how his creations hurt each other so brutally. And yet the creator of all things also made flowers and that wonderful smooth curve of Remy's behind. Like God spent extra time to make sure his reward for being a hero was justly served up on a silver platter for him. He could hear the words, '*Thank you, son.*'

He also heard it every time he saved someone's life or rid the world of a genuine bad guy. He'd never be able to tell anyone about that. Not ever. Not even Remy.

He touched his forehead to the cool tile and inhaled the steam, seeking to purge the morose thoughts.

Give me strength. What am I doing here?

These little events were popping up just like the unexpected things in the BUD/S training. His task was to just continue forward and endure, so that somehow, some day, it would all make sense. He hoped that day would come soon, because he wasn't very patient.

It was dangerous to cling to anyone, but if Remy wasn't here, he'd be outta Dodge and never come back. Yet, it was okay to cling to her, because she was strong and getting stronger. The more he showed he needed her, the more she delivered. It was sad admitting he truly began to love her *more* the day after she'd left him. He'd never thought she could be that strong— stronger than he was at the time.

And the first couple of times they met here in St. Helena, she put him off as well. She didn't want just the sex. Remy wanted the whole package. He could see that now. That's why she left. And she was afraid, too— afraid of becoming the kind of woman who was okay with watching her man sink lower into the abyss of alcohol and drugs. That wasn't for Remy. And because she got out, leaving him alone to sort through all that crap by himself, he'd been able to break free.

Did he deserve her? Would she tire of him when he wasn't strong? Would his limp bother her in time as it got worse? Would she grow weary of the surgeries that came to make it so his bones didn't fuse and the musculature would support them properly? He didn't want to be a cripple, disabled. He wanted to be whole for her.

The water was getting cold and she still hadn't come to get him. She was right not to join him.

He quickly soaped off with her bright pink fluffy scrubber and shampooed his hair with the lavender vanilla shampoo as he shivered in the ice cold water. He was washing himself under the protection of Remy's world, in her huge heart. He knew no one ever would love him the way she did. He also knew that no one else could love her back like he did, like he would the rest of his life.

You lucky bastard.

He turned off the shower and heard music playing on the other side of the door. He was curious, so dried off quickly, wrapped the towel around his waist, and turned off the light. As he opened the door, steam swirled around the room, staying to the ceiling and traveling several feet before disappearing. Through the mist he could make out candles—so many of them he wondered for a second if the place was on fire.

His eyes adjusted to the soft light illuminating objects here and there. Her bra was slung over a chair, and her panties dropped in a puddle on the rug. The music was soft, not anything he'd heard before, but something that would have been in a dream.

His gaze traveled to the bed and he saw her. Remy's long hair fell all around her shoulders as she lay against a mountain of pillows. She wore a red flowered silk robe, opened at the front, allowing just enough of her beautiful breasts to take his breath away.

He was afraid he'd spoil the dream as he stood there before her in his nakedness. But he had to tell her how beautiful she was. When he tried, he discovered he'd lost his ability to speak. Stepping toward the bed, he knelt on the coverlet, taking stock of the vision before him.

Her steady gaze acted like a homing beacon, drawing him up closer until he could touch her face and then blend his lips with hers as he crouched over her. He laid his body against hers, his head on her chest, and listened to the sounds of her life coursing beneath him. Her fingers lazily twirled through his hair as her chest rose and fell, taking him with her on the lullaby.

It all seemed so simple now, with his body separated only by the comforter. He peeled back the covers beyond her hips until he felt her warm flesh. He rested in the cradle of her arms for a few minutes, listening to her ragged breathing matching his own.

No barriers.

He savored the way her nipples twisted and knotted as he sucked her sweet flesh, dipping his head lower. His hands prayed between her thighs, and she parted them for him, allowing him to inhale her sweet arousal. Nothing was better than this, he thought.

I have the whole world, right here.

He wanted to be gentle tonight with her. Perhaps she knew, because she moved to her side then slid up and over his hip, on top of him. She adjusted herself to ride his groin, making gentle undulations like rocking a boat. His cock found her easily and she moved back and forth, shivering in the room's glow as he grew and pierced her lips to lodge deep inside her. Remy's fluttering eyelids and graceful arms, holding her hair atop her head, showed him how satisfying it was to have him seated at her soul. She savored every stroke until her moan drove him wild.

He battled her to try to get on top, but she insisted on her pleasure ride, keeping him safely tucked beneath her. Her knees hugged his hips. Her fingers laced up and down his chest as she bent, kissing him deeply, allowing her breasts to touch and warm him.

She arched backward, and his hands instantly went from her soft behind to the pillows of her chest. Her knees supported her elevation as she rose and fell upon his shaft, milking him gently, making his ears roar with anticipation.

When he began to feel her internal muscles clamping down, he slowed his hips but exaggerated the upward thrust so he was lodged against her cervix, which exploded in spasms out of control. She held her breath, grabbing his shoulders to brace for the oncoming storm.

Her long, rolling orgasm lasted several minutes, bringing a soft sheen of sweat to her upper lip. She sighed into his mouth, and he took everything he could. He found her bud, laid his forefinger against it, and rubbed then twisted it. He pressed her while he pushed deeper still, waiting for his spill to slow. Her moist body at last collapsed on top of him. Their breathing slowly returned to normal.

She started to climb off.

"Stay. Stay this way, Remy."

"All night?"

"Why not?" He smiled, looking at her puzzled expression. He drew the hair from her face and tucked it behind her ears. "Thank you. This was beautiful. This was exactly what I needed tonight."

"We both needed it. You are my touchstone, Derek. You make me want to give you anything you ask. I don't doubt a thing when you're here with me this way."

"You shouldn't doubt, because this is real, Remy."

She tenderly kissed him again, rocking against him and hid behind the veil of her long hair. Behind the curtain of her modest love he felt in every pore of his body, she whispered, "This is what I was made for."

He'd had the same thought earlier tonight in the shower. Whatever was to befall them both, together, they could handle it. He was certain of that now.

CHAPTER 14

THE COOKING SCHOOL was buzzing with rumors about the upcoming TV series. Remy heard many outrageous things, including the opinion that a bevy of Hollywood celebrities were going to descend on their little tourist town. Miss Bernstein confided in her that enrollment shot up as news of the series got out into the general public.

"It's been giving Admissions fits," she'd told Remy. "They don't know whether these kids are serious or looking to start an acting career."

Clearly, having Derek Farley, trained lethal athlete and super warrior, learning how to cook pies and pastries was good for the school.

She found friends in people who had ignored her previously. It amused her how popular she'd become. People were working to get closer to Derek by making nice with her. And that was okay, she told herself.

The last thing she wanted to do was rain on his parade. She allowed him the limelight when he wanted it and conspired with him when he needed a break from it all. They even devised several disguises so they could still stroll down Main Street hand in hand, without drawing a news crew. It actually started out to be great fun. The candy shop allowed her to use the rear entrance, giving her the employee all-access key to the second floor storage room. From there, they had to climb out a window onto the fire escape and make it to the fire access door outside her apartment. No one from the street could see them.

But she'd had to keep her window closed just in case someone recognized Derek.

Even the knowledge she and Derek were engaged made little difference to the chasers, who were relentless. He had a crowd of girls around him on campus, sometimes making it difficult for him to meet up with her.

Today was going to be the first day of promo filming. The real episode wasn't going to start production until nearly a month out, and would air just before their plans to attend the wedding in San Diego. That also meant Derek had to stop by the LA studios of the executive producer for some interviews with the local stations.

She rounded the side of the auditorium and slipped quietly through the large carved oak doors.

The din in the foyer was deafening. A line of young women getting their makeup done led from the auditorium arena entrance to the emergency exit at the end of the hall. Each of them wore the CCA's signature white chef's jacket, though Remy didn't recognize more than a handful as being real students. Several of the young ladies didn't have white blouses and black trousers, the school uniform, but instead wore their jacket over a skimpy bathing suit.

She was horrified.

None of the faculty was present, but several administrators were. Miss Bernstein was one of them, so she drew her aside.

"Where did all these ladies come from?" she asked the Assistant Admissions Director.

"The producers made all the arrangements. Not sure how it's done, but this is what they wanted." Her eyebrows nearly buried themselves in her scalp.

"Are they supposed to be students?" Remy asked.

Miss Bernstein shrugged and tossed her head about as if it had no importance at all. "It's only a promo, an ad, to get viewership. You know how it goes. Trying to sell the series."

Remy understood how ridiculous it would look to any serious chef, and didn't see how it could possibly enhance the well-known school's reputation.

Bernstein was watching the line, her arms crossed,

her fingers tapping on her upper arms. She began to chew her lower lip. "You think it's too much?" she finally blurted out, as if it took courage to do so.

"Yea, I think it's too much. It's unrealistic."

The Assistant Director threw her head back and laughed, nearly losing her dark-rimmed glasses. "Oh really? So you think those chef programs on television are real? It's all *staged*, Remy. Come on. You didn't know that?"

Remy watched the line of lovelies as if she could find her answer there, but then stepped back, cleared her throat, and whispered, "I'm sorry. I've got almonds or something making me cough. Would you excuse me?"

That simple trick gave her some privacy as she bolted into the ladies room, nearly in tears. She met another four girls doing their own makeup, chatting like they were dancers backstage at a burlesque show.

It was all wrong.

After pretending to need the restroom, she flushed and washed her hands, listening to the banter going back and forth.

"Honest to God, I've always wanted to fuck a Navy SEAL. I'm going to make sure to give him a big squeeze under the counter, right when the camera is rolling!"

The girls were overcome with tittering. Remy almost lost her breakfast—that nice granola and fruit yogurt Derek had made for her and helped her eat in bed this morning. They didn't know who she was nor did they appear to care.

She gave a pert smile as she dried her hands and exited the doors.

Away from the lines, Remy slipped down the side of the auditorium and came through the service entrance, which forked off in three directions. She guessed at the door and was rewarded as she walked into the auditorium just above the orchestra seating, midway.

Bright lights on the stage had the room nearly ten degrees warmer than usual. Derek was behind the demonstration counter, trying to stay composed, but sweat was dripping off his forehead. An artist was standing close by him, trying to reapply powder until Remy heard his familiar growl.

"Quit it! You're gonna make me sneeze."

That brought on some whispered disagreement from the crew, who apparently had heard this once or twice before. Suddenly, John McCormick appeared from the wings, ordering people around and demanding they cut some of the lights. He stood next to Derek and placed his arm around him.

"Now, Derek."

Remy understood full well what "making nice" was all about, and McCormick was a master at sweet talk.

But she couldn't wait for the result once Derek got wind of it.

Her fiancé gave some warning, shrugging off McCormick's arm and stepping to the side.

Someone in the darkened audience reminded him to stand where he'd been directed, so Derek pushed McCormick aside and resumed his spot. As the makeup artist came running to powder his forehead again, her SEAL hunk held out his hand, shouting, "Don't!"

The young woman stopped in her tracks and retreated to the shadows without a sound.

A couple of lights were turned off.

"Better, but not enough. I'm sweating like a suckling pig—you *do* say that here, don't you?" Derek barked.

Remy couldn't wait for the swearing to begin. She didn't have to wait long.

John McCormick might have been a smart chef and a good salesman and talent, but he didn't know the first thing about SEALs, Remy surmised. He slipped back to Derek's side and was going to drape his arm around him again, but before any part of him could touch Derek's shoulder, she heard the familiar, "Fuck off, or I'll kick your nuts."

Gasps erupted all around the set. McCormick was laughing, in spite of his miscalculation.

"I *love* it! Did you get that?" he asked the crew.

"Yessir we did. Not sure we can use it, though."

"We'll bleep it," McCormick said. He rolled up his sleeves and leaned into the demonstration counter, putting his body weight on his palms, and relieving it from the small of his back. And then he turned to Derek, all business.

"Now, Derek. That was funny, really funny, and will make a splash, if we can use it. I don't need much from you, but if we don't get through this little promo thingie here today, we're packing up and going home."

"Fine with me," Derek said defensively.

Someone in the darkness moaned.

"Look, think of what it will mean to thousands of veterans out there who will watch this segment and think, 'maybe I can get a job working in a kitchen, and do something really fun and creative like decorating cakes and making pies instead of frying hamburgers and fries or hanging out at the local pub.' You see what we're trying to do here?"

Remy could tell Derek was making choices in his head.

"It's for the veterans?" he asked.

"That's right, Derek. This will be inspiration. And yes, it's a little over the top—"

"What the fuck is over the top?"

"You'll see. All we've done is get you set up and

check the lighting. We haven't let in the ladies yet. That's when it gets fun."

Remy's stomach fell to her ankles. *Oh shit.*

"We're going to let the audience see how a big bad Navy SEAL—"

"*Former,*" Derek interrupted.

"Okay, yes, *former* Navy SEAL demonstrates his cooking skills."

Derek pinched some flour in the stainless steel bowl in front of him and let it drizzle from his fingers. "With flour," he said.

"Well, yes, this *is* a pastry show, after all."

"But you said I had no lines."

"That's right, you just make something up. The girls are going to watch you, trust me. There is going to be music overlaid so they aren't going to hear what you guys say to each other. You can talk about your favorite kind of popcorn for all I care."

Remy saw Derek was going to try, but McCormick hadn't convinced him he should be anywhere near the set. She held her breath as three beautiful long-legged ladies, each in a red or white or blue bathing suit with the chef's jacket barely covering their more than ample cleavage, joined Derek on stage. He acted like he didn't notice.

"Okay, so just pretend you're showing them something, just make small talk, and....here we go."

"This is the most ridiculous thing I've ever done," said Derek.

"Are you really a Navy SEAL?" asked the brunette wearing the red suit.

"*Was. A former* Navy SEAL."

"Focus on the flour, Derek. You're showing her how to do something."

Remy knew it wasn't going to work because Derek didn't like to take orders from someone he didn't respect. But she wasn't expecting what happened next.

Just as she'd told her friends, the blonde next to Derek slipped her hand under the counter and, from Derek's reaction, must have given him an ample squeeze.

Derek immediately threw the contents of the bowl, nearly four cups of flour, in her face.

CHAPTER 15

D EREK DIDN'T CARE if the whole program tanked
and they flunked him from CCA. He wanted to
help the school, but he didn't want to make a dime for
the stuffed peacock in the suit, John McCormick.

It didn't matter that McCormick thought he was
hilarious, or that the crew was furious with him
because of the mess he'd caused, or that he'd refused to
do another demonstration that day. He was glad Remy
appeared out of nowhere as he exited through the rear
of the stage, taking his hand and laying a lip-lock on
him that was way better than he'd ever dreamed. And
he could dream about some good ones, too.

He was here to resume some kind of a normal life,
not become some reality TV star, which is where he felt
he was being pushed. And it wasn't what they did in
the community, at least the good ones didn't. They
didn't make fun of their time in military service, and
that's what McCormick was doing. It was disrespectful.

He was a cartoon character of himself, playing a role he never wanted to play, falsely leading people on so someone could have a successful show.

"I nearly peed my pants," Remy had said that morning. "It was perfect!"

"I didn't like it too much," he answered under his breath.

"That's what made it so perfect. No hiding the fact that you were so out of your element, the audience will be able to *feel* your pain."

"No, she didn't squeeze me that hard. You squeeze harder, you know." He waited for her to catch his comment, and then he gave her a big hug when she giggled into a blush.

A day or two later, they gave him some choices, as far as demonstrations went. And they agreed to one of his requests to work with Remy on stage a bit later in the season. In the meantime, he would have to endure some of John's less than tolerable ideas, but he'd do it for the chance to work with Remy. That was all he cared about. He agreed to throw a little flour here and there, but refused to smear chocolate frosting on anyone's chest. That he could not do.

DEREK BEGAN WORKING for Horace Gerson at the Wet N Wild park, which was like the dark side of the moon from his culinary school courses or even the filming—

something he was entirely grateful for. He didn't feel naked anymore because he got to run around with Gerson's Remington long gun. Like an old friend, the extra weight didn't begin to match the relief it gave him having that puppy strapped to his back. There wasn't anything he couldn't hit dead-on if he had any kind of notice. He had his SigSauer and a hatchet attached to his utility belt for those quick moves. And Gerson had talked him in to wearing an extra KA-BAR, since Derek had left his in storage at San Diego.

He'd asked about using a cattle prod to help with animal control at the ranch, but Gerson laughed in his face. "Only on women if they need it."

Derek must not have hidden his shock well, because Gerson slapped him on the back and nearly sent him to the ground with his teeth embedded in the red dirt.

"Nah, I'm not that way. But I can't say as I haven't thought about it a time or two, if you get my drift."

Derek looked away to stop bursting into laughter. He didn't want to think the image funny, but it was.

"Seriously," the former SEAL said calmly, "only thing that you'd need to stop is the Buffalo. And if you hit them with a prod, they'd get so mad, you'd likely wind up dead."

"Gotcha," Derek answered just before they hit a pothole that took him four inches off the passenger seat.

At the base camp, Gerson was out of the Land Rover practically before it came to a stop. "I'm working on getting a storage container emptied so you can park your nice vehicle inside. Those animals are smart, and if they get a chance to show you their stuff, they'll pick out your ride exclusively and ram it until it's flat as a pancake."

"Thank you. I'm trying to make it last. Probably the last new truck I'll buy," Derek admitted.

"My suggestion, not that you need it? Get one mechanically sound but with lots of dents and scratches in it. Somehow, they seem to dislike the shiny things the most."

"Damn, they're smart." Derek's admiration for the beasts had been growing steadily ever since his first encounter the day he was hired.

"Yup, and straight from Hell, too. No conscience, or decency. They forget and run over their own young. Like I said, the most dangerous animal on the planet. Even worse than women!"

Whatever had left him vacant and hollow about the play-acting and the slice of stardom had been filled just smelling the sweat off this man, and hearing his stories.

It wasn't a surprise that someone so crusty and prepared for Doomsday would favor protecting and living with animals—even the most dangerous ones at that. It confirmed what he'd always believed, that a true hero doesn't kill. He saves things until his last dying breath.

Heroes weren't developed. They were made that way.

DEREK DECIDED TO have a talk with the crew before they did their next taping. He wanted them to understand a little of what he was about.

He brought a stack of his favorite books about the SEALs, their training, history, and some of the missions they'd done in the past, both ones that were successful and those that weren't.

John McCormick wasn't present that day, so Derek knew he had only a few minutes to get through to the crew.

"These are books I recommend. You can't have them because they are my personal copies and most of them are signed."

He tried to visualize what he wanted to say, and under normal circumstances he would have closed his eyes and done a meditation, but he didn't have the luxury of time. Over the next few seconds the scenes from his past became clearer, more vivid, and even painful.

"First, I want to say that I'm no hero. There are people out there right now who are the real heroes, doing better work than I did, helping to make this world a safer place. You don't hear about them, because that's the nature of what they do. They are like the controllers or stage managers who never get their shot on camera, unless there's a mistake made."

His heart was beginning to ache. He'd never tried telling his story to people who didn't know him.

"The purpose of what we do on the SEAL Teams is to make it so the war doesn't come home here to the U.S. We are out there doing things so you guys can make movies, run around, overspend, fall in love, buy new cars, and go shopping in the mall without fear." He caught himself.

"Well, at least it *used* to be that way."

He found several of the team nodding.

"But most of us living here don't have to worry about our freedoms being taken away or our schools overrun by bands of roving commandos, or bandits. We don't have to say good-bye to our children and worry their school will be blown up. It isn't always that way, but we're working on it."

He looked around the auditorium, pictures of famous chefs in white coats adorning the walls. Names of world-class restaurants decorated a banner draped over the back wall.

"Here, we get to learn how to make incredibly beautiful and tasty things for people who enjoy the luxury of a world class meal and have the money to pay for it. But I've seen kids eat rocks for dinner, or scrounge through our garbage bins behind the kitchen, hoping to bring something home to their families. Sometimes they're too proud to ask for the food we'd willingly give them. They don't want handouts. Or they don't want to be seen talking to us. They just want to not be hungry anymore, and they have the same basic need to help their families."

"I've seen mothers try to throw their babies at us when we're leaving town, asking us to take them to a safe place, a hospital. I've seen children's arms hacked off after our team gave out shots to help keep them from the diseases we've eradicated nearly a hundred years ago here. Terrible things happen to women and children in the war zones. Sometimes because they want to stay behind to help their men, but mostly they're used as human shields, where their lives are not respected. Casualties of war. It's hard to see. It must be impossible to see for you guys, living here in the land of plenty, in a place almost like Heaven."

He had everyone's attention, though several people squirmed. He would have to be careful with the brutal stuff.

"As for what I did, I didn't do anything but try to stop some of this Hell from spreading. I devised explosive devices to open doors that were barred to us, or to get rid of a truckload of enemy, or to form a diversion. I never did it for fun or because it was cool. I never did it for the money, and I never got any applause for it. I'm not ashamed of what I've done, because everyone I've sent back to the source deserved to go there. So the answer to the questions everyone wants to know is, yes, I've killed people. I'm happy to say I don't have the guilt of taking an innocent's life— that I know of. But I slept with, ate with, and cried with men who have and will be haunted by those terrible mistakes their whole life. There are just some things you cannot *unsee*."

The side door to the auditorium opened, and John McCormick stepped inside.

"We having a funeral or memorial service here folks?" he blurted out.

No one said a word. Then Derek spoke up.

"I just need five minutes, and then we can start. I'd like a volunteer this time. No more girls in skimpy tops, please."

Everyone in the room except John McCormick raised their hand.

CHAPTER 16

A S THE WEEKS went by, Remy noticed Derek's new-found interest in food growing. He sat in on other cooking classes and experimented with main courses he'd seen demonstrated. He was turning into a versatile, innovative, and smart chef. Her own little piece of the pie was looking very small in comparison.

He was consulted on anything the school did, since he was such a media draw. He sat for interviews weekly and had shaken off the gruff exterior, controlling his language. As they walked across the campus, he was addressed. She didn't mind that people weren't addressing her.

At first.

But the more the culinary school's ads were run on random TV stations, with their pictures of the flour fights and Derek standing with his big goofy grin, surrounded by beautiful women who obviously adored him, the more that little hardness began to grow inside her. She now understood she was beginning to feel jealous.

She was jealous that the whole world belonged to Derek. And who was she becoming? A sidekick? A pastry chef? Perhaps some day a bride? And then a mother? She was his manager, the support staff, the one who ironed his shirts and reminded him what time it was. Her schedule revolved around his—his interviews, his filming, his scheduled speaking engagements on behalf of the school, which sometimes took him out of town.

The school even gave him leeway to make up missed classes. He got personal private instruction, which she often attended. Derek was indeed special. How could she feel this way for someone she loved? To be jealous of his "specialness?"

Even their sex life suffered. Neither of them initiated their approach. They stopped surprising each other with little promises of liaisons, teasing and making little flirty talk. Things were more matter-of-fact and flat.

He'd told her they approved her joining him on the show, but that day hadn't happened. She believed him, but some days, she felt like everyone else came before she did. There were missed dates, broken dinner plans, and daytrips in wine country that had to be rescheduled. She was beginning to wonder why she lived in St.

Helena, one of the most picturesque places in the world that people spent thousands of dollars to visit, if she wasn't able to enjoy it with the one she loved.

"You sound a little blue, Remy," her mother said one day. "Are you planning the wedding at all? It's customary for the family of the bride to help."

She even forgot about the wedding some days. They had yet to set a date. "Mom, Derek is so busy. We just don't know what is going to happen from week to week. If we plan something, it could all change. Now they're talking about having Derek fly to places in Europe to meet celebrity chefs to make a European series out of it for next year perhaps."

"Well, who would have thought? Honestly, can't he just stay out of one part of your life?"

"Mom, what the Hell are you talking about?"

"Well, you made the decision to go up there and start a new life. It's like Derek followed you, and then completely took over. Have you ever talked to him about this?"

"He's being successful. No. Gosh, Mom, that would be horrible of me."

"Well, all I can say is it would be distracting as Hell for anyone to live with him."

"Mom, what do you mean? You can't be serious."

But Remy had actually thought the same things. At first it was a distant vision, but the more time went by, she wondered if there would be a day when Derek decided he didn't need her any longer.

After the call, she decided she'd go visit her grandfather, who was staying at one of the resorts for the weekend. Derek worked both Saturday and Sunday at the park, staying over Saturday night. She'd been invited, of course, but she needed time alone.

Before she dialed his cell, she examined her now-bare left hand. The little engagement ring had been nearly lost several times, so she stored it in her jewelry chest. Superstitious about changing the size, she left it intact as-is, just like she said she would. And she waited for Derek to notice. So far, he'd not said a word.

Harrison Bolt picked up the call on the first ring.

"Your mother has this habit of pre-warning me about a possible call from you. She's got a Sixth sense about these things."

"Hi Grandpa. I'm sorry she does that."

"Like she thinks I can't handle a call from you right out of the blue. My ticker is a Hell of a lot stronger than hers, if you ask me. While I was racing cars and making mine work overtime, she was watching soap operas to exercise hers. Mine's better used."

"I think so too. And for the record, we didn't have a disagreeable conversation."

"So the wedding's still on?"

Remy gulped air. "She said we'd called it off?"

"More or less."

"She takes things to their tragic end sometimes, and you know that, Grandpa. Things are fine. They're busy, but they're fine. Derek has really found his stride at CCA."

Her grandfather paused then asked her to lunch. "I've been eating at that Bistro place, and it's really good," he said.

"I know. They tell me every time I've been in there. And you've been dating, I hear."

"Nah, not really."

"And I'm not really getting married, either. You don't fool me. See you in twenty."

She chose a table by the front and heard her grandfather's approach in his Shelby before she saw him. If she'd been looking, she surmised, she could have just watched the dogs and tourists run for the sidewalk or follow the trail of road dust. He liked to rev the engine just before he shut it off, so the entire restaurant was well aware of his arrival. Several people stood and shook his hand while he made his way over to Remy's table.

It suddenly occurred to her that Derek and her grandfather had a lot in common. There was a bit of showmanship in Derek as well. The difference was that her grandfather relished and basked in it, while Derek tried to tell himself it wasn't who he was. She wondered about the collision course that might make for him some day.

"Dearie, I have to tell you you're looking rather fit, but perhaps too fit?" Bolt said as he carefully seated himself across from her.

"I'm not fat."

"I didn't say you were fat. But you're filling out."

She thought about the meals she'd prepared that Derek had missed. Many times she'd saved the main course for him to use for lunch the next day, but she'd eat the dessert. Maybe too many desserts.

"Hazardous work. It's all good. Derek likes it. He always thought I was too skinny."

"Well then, everything's okay." He ordered some white wine and asked Remy what she wanted, and she took iced tea. Then her grandfather ordered without looking at the menu. Being conscious of the comment he'd made, Remy ordered a wedge salad.

She folded her hands in her lap. Suddenly, she had an idea.

"Grandpa, why don't we go shooting?"

"Remington! What made you think about that?"

She shrugged, laughing at herself. "I don't know. I just thought of it. Thought it might be fun right now."

Harrison Bolt leaned over the table toward her and squinted. "Who in the devil are you wanting to shoot now?"

She laughed. It took a few seconds before Bolt broke into a smile as well. "All I can say is my Una used to tell me on the farm where she was raised if one of her girlfriends wanted to go shooting, it meant there was a fight brewing. It was a safer alternative than the real thing."

"Rest assured, I don't want to shoot Derek. I'm just a little out of practice."

"Well, I didn't bring anything with me. I'm so rusty I'd probably kill my car just getting it out of the trunk."

"And that would be a shame," she answered. She loved the irreverent way her grandfather played his life. She wanted to be just like him when she was eighty.

"It would be a damned shame. There ain't anything like a man and his car. That car makes me a much younger man, with plans to live forever. Brings back all the memories of the thrill of anything you can do with a car." He leaned forward and whispered, "Or anything you can do in the back seat of a car."

She nearly spit out her water. She wasn't as connected to any object like that. She was totally connected to Derek, though.

"Can I ask you something?"

"Shoot," he said, drawing on her over the plate.

"Why were you married four times, grandpa? Why not just once?"

He looked back at her with tears in his eyes. "Because, sweet Remy," he took her hand in both of his. "Your grandmother Una left me. If she'd have lived longer, there would never have been a Mrs. Bolt number two, three, or four."

She was suddenly sad for the years of love that Harrison Bolt would never have. And he was not lying to himself about it, either. He knew when the right person came along that he could make a decision for a lifetime.

"God intervened. I think he wanted her for himself."

CHAPTER 17

DEREK WAS GRATEFUL to be attending Cassie's wedding in San Diego. He was aware something was pulling them apart, and he wanted to fix that. Remy didn't complain, but he knew his crazy schedule cut into their personal time. In fact, there was hardly any personal time.

He was expecting her to say something like she did when he was off on deployments. His focus was on his work and on his brothers, even when he was home. It took him longer and longer to recover after each deployment. And then when he tore out his knee and broke his hip on that bad jump, overnight everything changed. He was beginning to recognize that he was either an off or an on guy. There was no in-between.

And that's where Remy lived most of the time.

He'd wanted that too. It wasn't turning out that way.

He glanced over at her as they sped down the freeway. "Happy?"

She gave him back a warm smile. "Ecstatic."

He nodded. "I get you. I haven't exactly been much fun lately, have I?"

He could tell she was pleased he'd noticed, but she was holding back. There was a little resentment building there, laced between the smiles.

"I just think you're making the most of the opportunities you've been given. These things run in waves. You strike while the iron's hot."

"You really believe that, Remy?" He knew she was full of good advice she never took herself. "You say the word, and I give all this up. We can go do something else."

"You are such a big liar! You're loving it. Go for it. I'm not going to be the one to stand in your way. It's your reward for working so hard to get well, for wanting to make a change. You did it. Enjoy it."

"I really came up here to prove I didn't need you. What a lie that was, right?"

She paused. "You don't need me, Derek. I don't want you to *need* me. I want you to *want* me, to want to be with me. But I don't think either of us should be dependent on the other. That's why I'm thrilled you've had all this success."

"Really?" He still thought she was making stuff up.

"Well, I'll like it more when they decide to replace

you with me. Then I'd be really happy."

They shared a laugh. It had been too long since that had happened.

THE LONG DRIVE gave him time to mentally adjust to the pace of hanging out with his brothers. Of all the things that he'd done while an active SEAL, the situation with Ray just before the breakup with Remy was his one regret. Ray had been a good friend. He'd started with him in the same BUD/S class, but Ray had bouts of asthma as a child, and when it came to the swim phase, meaning timed swims in the inlet or bay or in the lap pool, he developed pneumonia and had to be hospitalized.

Ray had been soft spoken and didn't mention how sick he really was until he passed out one day on a PT jog on the beach, collapsing at Derek's feet. He was hot and sweaty, shivering in his semi-consciousness. Derek carried him to the dorm where they had an ambulance waiting to take him away.

Everyone was worried it was Meningitis, which would have affected Derek as well, but Ray's tests came back negative. His former friend spent nearly eight months recuperating.

As happens often in the training, men get injured or sick, and they roll back to a later class. In Ray's case, it took an especially long time to get him hooked up with another group because of the Christmas holidays and some BUD/S staffing shortages so he could continue the next phase. Eventually he did, and he graduated with that class.

Afterward, he attended specialty school to become a medic, opting to take the year-long course only a few get lucky enough to take. So while Derek was already overseas on missions, Ray was still getting further training and had yet to deploy.

Derek believed Remy's story about Ray. All he wanted to do was apologize to his former friend, shake his hand and tell him they were square. It was the right thing to do. He knew Ray would appreciate him going out of his way, and knew if it was reversed, Ray would do the same for him.

Remy had arranged to pick up a white tux at the bridal shop just outside Coronado. The two of them had had some fun, finally, getting him measured. Of course Remy took some extra measurements that had nothing to do with the wedding, but they were fun and just what the doctor ordered.

All the other men in the wedding party were active SEALs, so last minute they decided to wear their whites. Sometimes the brides liked the uniforms. Sometimes they elected not to have them. Cassie couldn't make up her mind to the men decided for her. In Derek's case, it didn't matter because he was no longer active.

He was also looking forward to seeing Knudsen again. The old fart had been texting him dirty pictures he could get in a lot of trouble for with the Navy. Suddenly the pictures stopped when Knudsen got a new phone. It was no surprise to learn soon after that he'd finally gotten a girlfriend. Old Knudsen was reeled in as tight as could be. He'd make sure to razz the guy to the point of nearly picking a fight.

Seeing Cassie would be fun. She'd been a pest, but a cute kid. Now, her mother was another thing altogether. That one he'd have to be as careful with as some of the chemical agents he used. She was as unpredictable as anyone he'd ever met and liked to win at all costs. He remembered a Sunday picnic with some of the guys and the families when Remy's grandfather was in town visiting. She made a play for the old guy and it was the talk of the Teams for weeks afterward. He smiled recalling the clear lines between the men and the wives and girlfriends as far as their opinions of the little tryst.

"Whatcha thinking about?" Remy asked him.

"Your grandpa and Hildie. Remember that picnic when she—"

"Oh God, don't remind me. My mother was furious when she heard about it. Said he could have had a heart attack."

"Hey, some men can perform quite well in their

late seventies." He figured if anyone could, it would be Harrison Bolt.

"My mother still says Grandpa was never the same after that." Remy leaned back and crossed her arms and huffed. Derek knew she was pretending. When she couldn't hold it any longer, she burst into a giggle, and Derek joined her.

"I'm going to tell your mother," he teased.

"You'll do nothing of the sort."

"Someone said he was back in St. Helena again a few weeks ago."

"Yes, we had lunch. I think he's looking to make this a permanent home."

"Well, I'll bet that will make most the ladies in the Shady Oaks retirement home start wearing more makeup and getting their hair done."

Good for them.

"He know about the engagement?"

He saw Remy darken, and then glanced at her hand, which was missing the ring he'd bought her.

"You took it off."

"I didn't want to lose it. And you seemed to be so busy, I just thought we'd revisit the whole decision when you had more time."

"That doesn't mean you've changed your mind?" The traffic was getting thicker as they entered the outskirts of the LA basin. He had to keep his eyes on the road, but he stole quick glances. She was struggling with something.

"This would be a helluva time to tell me you've decided not to marry me, Remy. Right before this big gathering and all."

When he checked her expression, he saw tears rolling down her cheeks.

"Sweetheart," he whispered as he took her left hand in his. "Let's stop for coffee."

"I'm fine."

"I'll be the judge of that, but we're stopping."

They pulled into a coffee shop. It felt good to stretch his legs and back. There were nearly three hours to go. They'd be there just after nightfall. Remy headed for the restroom while he ordered and then took a table in the corner.

He wondered how long she'd been without the ring and why he never had noticed it before. Perhaps it was just a recent thing.

Remy returned from the ladies' room just as the barista was calling his name, so she stopped and helped him by carrying her own drink.

He was going to let her go first.

Remy rimmed the top of her coffee mug and bit her lower lip. She stared out the window and then back into the crowd seated all around them. She watched her fingers tap on the tabletop, and then she stopped.

"Derek, I've not been wearing a ring for over a month now. It was coming off all the time and I worried I'd lose it. You and I just never talked—"

"That's my fault."

She searched his eyes. He knew that statement had been important to her.

"I'm going to fix that," he said.

"Remember that discussion we had about needing and wanting?"

He did, and nodded *yes*.

"I'm at this funny place again." She examined the top of her cup. Still looking down, she continued, "Derek, I don't want to interfere with your career or your future. I don't want to feel like I'm the stone around your neck."

"Nonsense. What do I have to do to convince you?"

"Just be you. But perhaps make *us* a little bit more of a priority. I can handle a lot. I learned to do that when you were overseas. This is harder, because you're home at night, but sometimes, you're still not here. Like when—"

He didn't like hearing this. "You're wrong, Remy. I'm doing this for us."

"I just want the truth, Derek. I can make a good wife. I can keep my side of the bargain. But I got to feel like I inspire you in some fashion, like when we first got together and earlier this summer when we got together again. That intensity is what I want. But I only want it if you do too. Otherwise, we're wasting our time."

Was he wasting his time? He'd been here before, just like she said. That time he didn't pay enough attention. That had been the wrong decision. This time he had the chance to do it right.

"Baby, no worries on that score. I'm here for the long haul. Like I said earlier, you just say the word, and we'll go live in a yurt somewhere in Wyoming and raise rabbits or something. Whatever you want. I don't need any cooking show, and I don't need a certificate from the school to know I can cook or to cook for us."

"No need to go to Wyoming. Why, I could just move into one of Wet N Wild's glamping tents and you could sing me cowboy songs while we listen to the Cape Buffalo mate in the distance and watch the stars all night long."

He'd made the mistake of describing the sounds the buffalo made during that ritual. It wasn't even slightly romantic. "Yuck."

She gave him back an honest smile and then started to giggle.

"Okay, I'm game. What is it?" He was intrigued.

"I was just thinking about Grandpa and Hildie."

That seemed to break the ice. He held her hand, kissed it. "I apologize. You're right. I've been preoccupied. You'll see. I'm going to make some changes."

"Thank you, Derek."

"Only thing I need to know is do you want the Fort Ross platform or the Nairobi one?"

CHAPTER 18

REMY THOUGHT DEREK was stunning in his white tux. He'd developed a deep tan working at the park and the heavy equipment he operated didn't hurt his shape any. His slim waist and hips were the perfect build for wearing white. It wasn't going to be dress whites like the other active SEALs, but he belonged right up there next to every one of them.

Several times during the few days prior to the wedding there had been gatherings on the beach with SEAL Team 3. Everyone who could brought their kids and spouses. She knew some of them, but most her former friends had been wives and girlfriends on SEAL Team 5.

In each crowd, she searched for Ray's face and never saw it. She was steeling herself, trying to imagine how she would feel seeing him again. He'd just gotten back from deployment the week before. Perhaps he was getting some much-needed downtime before he was ready to jump into the crazy antics of the Brotherhood again.

Derek introduced her to Kyle Lansdowne, Pete's LPO, and his wife, Christy. Kyle was also in the wedding party.

"Aren't you glad the men are in the wedding, and we get to stand down?" Christy whispered to her as the men engaged in a private conversation.

"I've never been in a wedding before, but you're right. Not complaining here."

Christy smiled and looked her straight in the eyes. The woman was gorgeous, and smart in so many ways. She was every bit the leader that her husband was. It was legendary on the teams. Remy was sad that Derek hadn't had that kind of leadership on Team 5.

"So I hear congratulations are in order. I say good on you for two counts."

"Thanks, but why the double congrats?"

"It takes a strong woman to stay with a man when he's hurting, and I understand you did that. Takes just as much to leave them when it's all wrong. But then you let him come back."

Remy knew what she wanted to say and wasn't sure how she'd take it. "That's because I love him, Christy. I'm only just beginning to learn how I can show it."

"I get it. I truly do. Good on you. Derek's a lucky man."

Christy gave her fiancé an up and down that wasn't sexual. Then she shook her head. "Pastry chef?"

"I chose it. He followed me up there."

"But pastry chef?"

Remy shrugged. "You know about the cooking show?"

"Oh. My. God. We couldn't believe it. Everyone down here loves that show. He's perfect for it."

"That's exactly what I told him, too."

"What did you tell me?" Derek said, coming up behind her and giving her a kiss on the neck.

The gesture was something she'd missed, and her eyes welled up with tears. She slowly turned to face him with his hands still around her waist. She rose to tiptoes and kissed him, then whispered, "I told her that you work wonders with your chocolate spatula."

He inhaled and focused on her lips, pulling her into him tight. "Darn. I left that wonderful implement at home. Perhaps we could improvise?"

"I'm game."

"So am I."

REMY ACCOMPANIED DEREK to the rehearsal and dinner on the eve of the wedding. The groomsmen were threatening to send Pete to Alaska, like they had done to one of their buddies, who didn't get back in time for his own ceremony. Hildie, Cassie's mother, somehow got wind of the discussion, nearly raised a scene, and demanded they stop talking about it. She was, as she usually was, drunk, and a mean drunk at that. Knudsen was the only person who could control his older sister, but he'd been MIA. Remy was going to do what everyone else was and avoid her.

Remy discovered Ray stealing glances in her direction, and she abruptly turned away, looking for someone else to talk to. But up until their meal, Remy could feel the SEAL's eyes on her. She didn't want to encourage anything private between them, and didn't return his gaze. But she knew by the way he was acting that he was fully available. He came alone, and he always stood facing her. No matter how many times she turned, he was there. Derek never seemed to notice.

Ray and Pete's parents also attended the dinner. Remy was assigned the seat next to Mrs. Carlson.

"You know, Ray used to talk about you all the time when he and Derek were friends. I never could figure out what happened between the two of them. They used to be so close," Ray's mom whispered.

Both of them looked in Derek's direction. He was laughing at one of Kyle's stories. Christy sat beside him with their oldest child, Brandon, who was in early grade school. He was a carbon copy of his dad.

Remy answered the woman, "They go through so

much. I can never figure any of that out, to be honest." It wasn't quite truthful but was a safe answer. "I think Derek has missed his friendship as well, so perhaps they'll get a chance to talk."

"You think so?"

"It's just a guess, Mrs. Carlson."

"He's very fond of you, Remy. You made quite an impression on him just before he left."

Remy's back went stiff. That was not something she wanted to discuss, let alone hear.

Ray's mother added, "He told me to keep it quiet, but I thought *you* should know."

Remy didn't like where the conversation was going. "You should have honored that request, Mrs. Carlson. He told you that in confidence. It should have been kept that way."

"I understand. I just want him to find a nice girl who will make him happy. Some day, when you have a son, you'll feel the same way."

No, thought Remy. *I won't be that kind of a mother at all.*

Adjacent the restaurant was a dance hall populated by a couple dozen senior couples. She was standing at the side, looking for Derek, and began watching Christy dance with Brandon. One of the older gentlemen asked her to dance.

He twirled her around the dance floor with ease.

She'd taken classes in high school, which had been one of her mother's requirements, and everything came back to her. She remembered the Saturday night dance hall back home and the sweaty palms of all the other nervous kids whose parents insisted on ballroom lessons. But she was enjoying herself right now. Her dance partner, while being well over seventy, was agile and classically trained. It was always a joy to dance with someone who knew how to lead, and he did.

Several others from the wedding party joined in. Then Remy noticed the bride draped over Derek, who looked like he wanted to be anywhere but there. She could tell he was searching the crowd for Pete or anyone to help relieve him.

Cassie's mascara had begun to streak. She was touching Derek's face, then leaning her head into his chest, clinging to him sloppily. Derek held on to her so she wouldn't lose her balance and take him with her. She looked wounded, and in pain. Remy felt embarrassed for her, and hoped her fiancé would get her home for a good night's sleep.

She was asked to dance again by another of the senior crowd, but this time had difficulty keeping up with the salsa number being played. She eventually got into the rhythm and then it felt good to move around. She caught Derek, now free of the clingy bride, watching her, so she poured on a little more flair, moving her hips and turning her head from side to side. She loved to dance for him.

Each time she turned, he was there, leaning against the doorway, his legs casually crossed, hands in his pockets with his head cocked at an opposite angle. She focused on his lips and moved faster when she saw his huge smile and noticed his need to adjust his stance, which meant only one thing.

He'd gotten a hard-on.

She ran to him after the music stopped.

"You are a vision, aren't you?" He bent down and gave her a kiss. She wanted more.

"Come dance with me," she asked and grabbed his hands.

"I don't dance."

"Yes, you do." Remy yanked, dragging him toward the dance floor.

"I like to watch, but I don't dance."

"Then come out to the center, and watch. Just be in the music," she insisted. To her surprise, he agreed.

It was not a dance tune she recognized, but it had a fast disco beat she could improvise. He moved just enough so as not to be accused of being a pole, and he followed when she reached out. She put his arms around her waist and gently encouraged him to rock his pelvis in tandem with her own. She could feel him laughing behind her, and it warmed her heart.

Several dances later, they said their good-byes and like most of the wedding party, left for the hotel to rest up for the big day tomorrow. He caressed her thigh the whole drive back. She had unzipped his trousers and was fondling him, which caused him to veer several times. She wondered if they'd make it back to the room in time. She had no willpower, but Derek got them safely to the privacy of their room.

Undressed and in bed, he whispered, "Remy, I loved watching you dance."

"You were a great sport, Derek. Did you enjoy it?"

He scrunched up the side of his face. "I wouldn't exactly call it enjoyment, but I'm glad I tried. You were the star tonight."

"We can dance some more, if you like," she teased.

"No thank you. I have other plans. I just wanted you to know how beautifully you move."

"I liked dancing for you, Derek. I like moving with you," she said as she raised her pelvis to meet his. She added, "Ahh, and I love this."

"Me too."

"Nothing better," she said to his eyes.

"Nothing better, forever, Remy. Forever."

CHAPTER 19

DEREK HADN'T SLEPT much. Their lovemaking had been satisfying, but something else was worrying him. Lying on his back, he wondered what tomorrow would bring. Though Remy was softly sleeping at his side, he felt alone, as if he was about to embark on an adventure of some kind. But that adventure was a mystery to him.

Perhaps he was irritated he couldn't find the space to talk to Ray, he thought. He felt ashamed for poor Cassie and wondered if this marriage would wind up a train wreck like so many of the SEAL marriages. There wasn't a person on the planet without demons of some kind, but he didn't like to see Knudsen's niece lack the control to hide them.

Knudsen!

Where was his best friend?

Derek had spent nearly a week away from all the pressures of the show and the heavy class load he was taking. That he didn't miss. But he did miss the animals and Horace, and he knew the poor man was probably staying up all day and night to fill in for Derek's work. They'd nearly finished the emergency pen for the buffalo, just in case there was a fence breach. Horace would do the last bit while he was gone.

He expected he'd fit in better once he got to San Diego. Kyle had talked to him about trying out again or asking for a second chance on his team, but Derek wasn't ready for that. On Team 3 his handicap would always be a factor. He just wanted to forget it even happened, and attending classes or standing up reading a cue card didn't require anything physically from him.

Once again, that annoying feeling that he didn't fit in nagged him. Perhaps that's what was keeping him up. His leg, which had left him free from pain ever since he landed in St. Helena, now throbbed. He wondered if it was all in his head.

They dressed, and Remy accompanied him while he joined the other Groomsmen at the chapel. The fall day was warm, like it usually was in Coronado, but had that bite in the air that hinted of some wind and perhaps rains to come.

He'd attended many weddings at this chapel over the years on the Teams, and most of that time, he'd been misbehaving, so he didn't remember any of them.

Now, dressed in all white, it was almost a dress rehearsal for his own wedding some day. That was a topic he needed to discuss with Remy. It had taken him too long to realize what her waiting must feel like. He didn't want to push her away again, just from his lack of attention. He was going to make it right, including the ring, and do it as soon as they got home.

Kyle shook his hand, looking handsome and fit for an old guy.

"I know what you're thinking. A little tight here in the stomach, right?"

Derek had missed the tiny paunch. But he knew better than to think Kyle was out of shape.

"Don't see a thing, Lansdowne. You still look pretty lethal to me."

"And you're a fuckin' liar, too, but I like it."

Fredo, which wasn't his real name, the explosives expert on Kyle's team, grabbed his arm. "Faraway, I thank Jesus every day she found you."

He'd always liked Fredo, who'd been raised in some tough neighborhoods and fought his way to becoming a SEAL. He'd mentored under him when he could, since Fredo was an old guy too.

"Hey Fredo. Good to see you, man. And I don't know what the hell you're talking about."

Kyle stepped in to explain. "He was the backup in case Cassie couldn't find you." He followed it up with a wink.

"Ah. Well, way I hear it, she wanted an all-SEAL contingent, so it should have been you." He pointed to Fredo.

"Holy Moly, no. If you weren't the groom, you needed to be right next to him. You know that about Cassie, right?"

Unfortunately, he did. "Poor kid."

"Damaged little bird," Kyle whispered. "But she has good taste in men. Pete is a great addition and a solid guy."

Fredo whistled. "Oh boy. He'll be working hard with that little one."

"Well, we're here to make her day memorable, in a good way," said Derek.

"You got it. We're delivering on that promise, too. All the way," agreed Kyle. "Besides, this is also for Pete, and he'd do the same for any of us."

"Speaking of such things, understand you and Remy are back together." Fredo's forehead bore several layers of creases above his unibrow and dark eyes.

"Yea, by some miracle." Kyle had forgotten how fast the news traveled, even from Team to Team.

Fredo came closer. "You and Ray?"

"Working on it." That was all he was prepared to say, and gave the signal the subject had to change.

Pete entered the little room followed by his brother,

Ray. Derek made eye contact with both of them immediately. Ray gave him a nod of respect.

Some instructions were given, and all the extras, including Fredo, were ushered out. Pete was getting congratulatory slaps on the back and someone brought some Bourbon, which was passed around. Ray slipped past several of the men to join Derek as they passed the bottle back and forth a few times before the others objected.

Without looking at each other, Ray began. "So I guess it's about time we had that talk."

"I'm all right, if you are, sport." Derek worked to make his voice sound calmer than he really was. The Bourbon was helping.

"That's not what I heard."

"A lot's happened while you were away. And how was losing your cherry?" Derek turned to face Ray to see how his comment registered.

"Fuckin' hated it. Can't understand why you didn't talk me out of it. But it was okay. We were ready for Hell, and we got a good dose of it. And yup, I got that fuckin' message about Remy too. Made my tour even more special." He looked down at his shoes and then gave Derek the return stare but wasn't as casual about it. Something dark lurked there. He looked a bit dangerous.

"I'm not going there, brother. Whatever happened,

it's all in the past, or at least that's how it is for me." Derek wondered about Ray's attachment to Remy, and he could see the rivalry between two men who perhaps loved the same woman was going to get in the way of their friendship, unless they both worked very hard.

"If she was still available when I got back, I'd have looked her up. But I'm sure she's told you, nothing happened, Derek."

He was thankful for the honest admission. "Thanks, man. That means a lot to me. I was a dumb fool."

The bottle came around again, and Ray grabbed it, handing it first to Derek. "You were that, my friend. A damned shame, too."

Derek presented the bottle to Ray's solar plexis, rather hard. But none of the liquor spilled, so all was well.

And with that gesture, they were on even terms again. Time would tell if the friendship would really return. But Derek was satisfied, for now.

DEREK STOOD BESIDE Kyle and soaked in the whole ceremony, glancing back and forth at Remy. She'd not taken her eyes off him since he'd made his entrance and turned to watch the bride enter the chapel. Ray was right to be a little in love with her. Maybe he was a lot in love with her. It could happen. He hadn't realized

Ray had spent that much time with her, but she'd been around when he was overseas, so yes. And he totally missed all of it. She was a prize and Derek had not been paying attention. He would not make the same mistake again.

Cassie and Pete danced down the aisle after the ceremony, and he wished them luck, like all of them did who knew how hard it was going to be. It was a serious commitment made without knowing all the facts, just like signing up. Just like life, he thought. But if they didn't quit, just like in the training, they'd make it. Just like you didn't have to love what you did all the time to be a good SEAL. You just had to pay better attention than the enemy.

He was supposed to walk down with one of Cassie's rather buxom friends, dressed in light chiffon and clutching his arm inappropriately. So he stopped partway down the aisle, leaned over and grabbed Remy, bringing her along too.

The audience loved it.

What a fuckin' showman I've become.

HE'D BEEN PEPPERED with questions about his career choice.

"Pastry chef?" He must have heard that question twenty times in the first half hour.

"You add any of your secret juice to make the

dough rise? Blow anything up yet, Faraway?"

He didn't mind being the butt of jokes.

"You guys should come up. I'll take you to Wet N Wild, where I work part time. This owner is a former Team 5 guy."

"You got a water slide in wine country?" someone asked.

"No, it's not like that. They have these Cape Buffalo, the meanest animals in the world. They run over things, run in herds. Incredible animals."

"You work in a zoo?"

"No. It's called glamping. The tourists come visit the animals and stay outside in these nice tents with heated mattresses. And I cook, believe it or not."

"They pay to have *you* cook, Faraway?"

In the end, the conversation always came back to his TV show. After all was said, the only thing most of his former mates would remember was that he got to do interviews on TV stations and work with pretty girls. They'd all seen the promos, and asked how many of the girls hit on him.

For the first time, Derek no longer felt he fit into his former community. Maybe it was because he was the injured one and had to deal with more issues there. Or, because he'd had to stretch beyond what he'd been trained, to adapt to a crazy world back home—the place they were fighting to save. But whatever the reason, he was glad he'd left and started his new life up north. He would never have gotten well seeing things he couldn't do, feeling like he was second class.

He looked over the crowd to find Remy and didn't see her. But Cassie found *him*.

The bride made little dance steps in his direction, grabbed his arm, and pulled him out onto the floor. It did no good to protest.

"Cassie, come on. You know I don't dance."

"That's B.S. Derek. I saw you dance last night."

He was surprised she was even conscious. "Then you *know* I can't dance."

She wrapped her arms around him and tried to barrel dance with him dirty. He disentangled himself, anger building.

"This is not cool. I'm not going to dance with you unless you behave. You're the bride, for Chrissakes."

"I thought I made my intentions known years ago."

"Like when you were fifteen? You think that counts?"

"Come on. Move a little bit so this doesn't look like a lecture. You're embarrassing me, Derek."

He went along with her request, lightly holding the small of her back but resisting her advances to dance close. "You're embarrassing yourself. You'll hate yourself some day. Don't do this. It will ruin your life." He wanted to say something about her mother, but dared not to. He didn't want to make a scene, out of respect for Knudsen.

"And by the way, where the Hell is your uncle?"

"I think he's coming late. He said the vineyard up there had a little accident, and there was a fire he was helping to put out. He goes way back with the Jacksons."

"He should have called me."

Cassie smiled up at him with her dreamy eyes. She could be pretty if she wasn't so dependent. He hoped that the passage of time would be good to her, because she was headed for a cliff in about ten years, he thought.

"He didn't want to spoil my big day, Derek. He knew I wanted this."

"This?"

"You and me. Dancing in front of all these people. Everyone knows."

"Knows what?"

"You were my first love, Derek, and—"

He stopped abruptly. "Jeez, Cassie. I never touched you. Don't go saying things like that."

"Oh, I know that, but I'm just having a little bit of fun."

Now Derek had changed his mind. Cassie was a full blown Bridezilla and would turn into her mom before poor Pete returned from his first deployment.

What a mess.

He was more than glad the music ended and without saying anything further, made a beeline for the nearest exit.

And that's where he saw Remy and Ray together, sitting, holding hands on a bench in the rose garden. It looked pretty damned romantic to him.

He turned to retreat back into the crowds at the reception and ran straight into Hildie. The impact surprised her, causing her drink to splash over her neck and chest. Derek was furious with himself.

Knudsen's sister frowned at first when she inspected the damage. But as her eyes rose to lock with his, she broke out into a wide smile, her horse teeth making her look like a twin to Knudsen. She laughed. It actually was more like a cackle, and it immediately drew attention.

"I'm sorry, Hildie. Let me get you something for that." He tried to get away, but she tugged his hand.

"No worries, sailor. I'd have slapped anyone else, but coming from you, I'm rather flattered." She blinked as if she'd lost her train of thought. "I think I'm flattered, anyway."

"Look, let's get you to the kitchen to find a dishtowel. So sorry. I hope I didn't ruin your dress."

He knew he was attracting attention. But he wanted to get her some place where she wouldn't cause a scene.

God dammit, Knudsen. Could really use you.

He put Hildie in one of the female catering staff's charge and exited the hall.

The afternoon had grown warm. He was angry at how normal it looked and sounded, with the birds chirping and the bright pink flower vines covering the front of the hall. He inhaled, trying to clear his head. He was not a quitter, but if Remy hadn't traveled with him, he'd have left right there and driven all the way back to St. Helena. The San Diego area, with all his history there and his former life, felt oppressive.

Now that he'd caught Remy perhaps in a lie, did that mean she was gone too? Why didn't he see the signs she was drifting from him again? Nothing around him fit. Everything seemed to be spinning out of control.

His cell rang.

"Knudsen, you dumb fuck. Where the Hell are you?

"Derek, we have big problems up here. I've been at Jackson's, and this fire came through the vineyard so fast we couldn't stop it from jumping up the ridge. The damn thing is spreading, and no one has anything to battle it. There are winds making it much worse than we first thought. We need men. I need you ASAP."

"Sure, I'll be right up there in as fast as I can. I'm at Cassie's reception right now. I'll just change and drive on up."

"No, Derek, you don't understand. You gotta get on a next plane. Have someone else drive your Hummer. We can't wait for you."

"Is it that serious? How big is the fire?"

"Turn on the news, man. There's not just one fire. There are eight. And they're all around and closing in on St. Helena."

CHAPTER 20

R EMY WAS GOING to head back to find Derek. She'd given Ray a good-bye hug, and of course, that's when Derek came running around the corner. She was shocked at his hateful expression.

"I don't have any time for this crap, Remy. And Ray, you and I will speak *later!*"

He began fumbling in his pocket for something.

"Derek! What's gotten into you?" she asked. She could smell the sweat and adrenaline blowing off him. He looked like he was about to explode.

"There's a fire up north, and I'm taking a plane back." He threw his keys, including the motel room key at her. "I'm sure loverboy here wouldn't mind taking you back to the hotel. I'll find someone to give me a ride to the airport."

"Hey—" Ray started to come to her defense.

"You better stay away, Ray," Derek shouted. "I'm not in the mood. But trust me, this time we'll have it out."

"A fire? Where?" she asked.

"Everywhere. Just talked to Knudsen, and he said it's been all over the news. I spoke to Horace, and so far the park is okay, but it won't be if the wind shifts. It's huge and headed right for town."

"Oh my God. Let me come with you, Derek." She would worry about the misunderstanding later. Right now, she wanted to go be by his side.

"I don't want you to go. You stay down here, where it's safe. I'll call when I can."

With that, he flew through the doors and disappeared. Remy picked up the keys she'd dropped, unprepared for the events unfolding and Derek's state of mind. He'd gotten it all wrong. And now he was headed straight for danger.

She declined Ray's offer to accompany her to the hotel. She found Kyle and Christy discussing something. The music had stopped, and people had turned on a local television station.

—and we're getting this just in, the two fires on the backside of Hampton's Ridge have now combined, and they're headed right for the town of St. Helena. The wineries are now the only thing separating this raging torrent from the town itself. But with no rain in sight and the wind continuing to be so strong, none of the bombers can fly, due to visibility issues.

Kyle addressed her. "Christy and I talked, and I'm going to meet Derek at the airport. I'm rounding up a few of the guys, and we'll go help out."

"Where's Derek?" she asked.

"He left already."

Remy's hopes sank. Christy put her arm around her shoulder.

"Look, I gotta ask you. Are you familiar enough with the Hummer to drive it back? Because you could stay here with Christy and the kids," asked Kyle.

"Yes, Remy, why don't you stay? Not a good idea to get caught up in all that. They're evacuating people and—"

"But I want to go help. I don't want him to go up there without support."

"Not this time, Remy," Kyle said without an ounce of emotion. "They need emergency workers. They're calling up everyone. So we're going as volunteers. He doesn't want to worry about you, so I think it's a better idea for you to stay put."

"Thanks, perhaps I'll get as far as my folks and stay there. It's about half way anyway."

"Good. Now, I gotta go." Kyle kissed Christy and promised an update when he could. Fredo followed him shouting names off as he tried to catch up to Kyle's full out run.

Cassie was sitting in a stupor, drinking the last of

her champagne. Remy felt sorry for the young bride, her new beau at her side, trying to console her. Several of the wedding party had been dashing out the door, removing their jackets and obviously making plans to join Kyle and Derek up north.

Ray appeared behind her. "I guess we really blew it, then. I'm so sorry, Remy. I truly am."

"I've been an idiot, Ray. A complete idiot." Tears streamed down her face, but her resolve was firm. She thought he might understand. "The most important person in my life has just left to go be a hero. It was what he was made for. The last thing I need to do right now is to sit back and watch."

"I get it. You need any help with anything, just call."

"Don't hold your breath, Ray. Being with Derek, loving him the way I do, is not a spectator sport. It's the only thing in the world that means anything to me. I've got to go lend whatever support I can."

"But you don't know how to fight fires."

"I can drive a big truck, a tractor, and I can shoot. That's more than most women can do."

She picked up their clothes at the motel on her way out of town. Derek's shirt brought tears to her eyes as she held his collar up to her nose. She put his flip flops back in their bag, along with his Hawaiian swim trunks and the two pairs of red, white and blue boxers. She took his shaving kit, deodorant and the cologne she'd bought him from the shelf in the bathroom and placed them lovingly in her makeup bag and zipped everything up in the duffel bag.

She turned after tossing the strap over her shoulder and examined the messed up bed that had been such a happy scene last night and this morning. She wanted to remember how it felt to be here with him, in case it would never happen again.

That's a ridiculous thought. We deserve more than that.

But as she started the truck and began her trip out of Coronado, crossing over the bridge with the view of all the ships below in the bay, she knew that even though she'd been pretty damned lucky in the past, there were never any guarantees. Whether it was the fire or the misunderstanding, they had two strikes against them.

She was going to do everything in her power to make sure neither of them interfered with the life she intended to live with Derek. Nothing would stop her now. She was not a quitter, and she'd never stop loving him, no matter what.

CHAPTER 21

PLANES WERE BEING diverted to Sacramento and Petaluma airports. Derek's was the last commercial flight allowed in to Sonoma County. The Napa airport had been closed since the morning. Kyle, Fredo, and several others from Kyle's team had joined him. Two of the guys were medics.

As they flew their approach to land, the Team saw the fire jump the six-lane freeway, finding a small mobile home park sufficient fodder to spread to the adjacent shopping center within seconds. No one said a word. They knew there would soon be a boatload of casualties.

If CalFire had the right equipment available, he and Fredo could assist with setting backfires to help divert the fire, which had now merged from five separate ones, to one that had already burned many homes in Santa Rosa. And the backside of it was headed right for St. Helena. He hoped the range between held, as it was the only entrance left to Wet N Wild.

As they deplaned, the smoke was already strong enough to instantly irritate their eyes. With the relentless hot wind blowing, flakes of grey ash the size of his little fingernail fell everywhere like snow.

Behind them, as they entered the small terminal, their plane took off. People who were stranded in the airport and wanted to leave threw up their arms and yelled at the service desks in protest.

The uniformed attendant was as frustrated as his unruly crowd. He probably had a family to go home to, just like they did.

"Ladies and gentlemen, we have to get the plane away from the ash and smoke or it will be too damaged to use."

Kyle frowned and turned to one of his men. "That right?"

The tall medic shook his head. "Nah, they want to save the plane. They'd let the airport burn, but not the plane."

Derek's thought was *what about the people?*

They were relieved to find the Suburban they'd reserved was still there.

"I was about to close up," the skinny red-headed kid behind the counter said. The contract says you're to avoid any hazardous area, but that's kind of hard since we've just been declared a disaster. But you know.

Common sense."

After everyone loaded up, Derek headed up and over a back road he knew about that ran along one of the wineries next to a Catholic convent. Fire had crested the ridge to their right, and was going to come down toward the freeway again.

"Where the fuck's all the emergency workers?" someone asked.

Nothing was in the air, no boride bombers. They heard no sirens, saw no fire trucks or police vehicles with sirens. It was like the fire was consuming everything in its path, and people were just scrambling to get out of the way fast enough. But the lack of rescue vehicles was the eeriest sight Derek had ever seen. That meant everyone was completely on their own. No one was going to come help save a bunch of scared animals and a crazy zookeeper with a peg leg.

He left a message for Knudsen, letting him know where he was headed and apologized for leaving the Jacksons without help.

Once they got to the ridge, they looked back at the devastation. Several subdivisions of expensive homes were fully engulfed, and yet, there were still cars coming out of those streets. He could see people running after pets, and several vehicles raced down the expressway with household items strapped to their roofs on fire.

But over the ridge, his heart sank. The valley floor, usually sprouting lush green rows of vines, could not even be seen. All they saw was grey smoke and occasionally a bright orange flash as a house or some structure burst into flame. It was obvious people left, leaving everything behind because they barely had time to save themselves.

He'd driven the road many times, picking up guests from Santa Rosa or bringing in supplies, which was lucky. Otherwise the winding ridge road would have been impassable.

"I'm reading to NIXLE texts and they've got a triage set up at the Calistoga Fairgrounds. That far away?" Kyle asked.

"I'll take you there first, but yes, it's about twenty miles from the camp."

"Then you take us to the camp. I don't see any requests for anything other than water tankers and supplies for the fire crews. They got them coming from all over, it looks like."

One of Derek's passengers asked how many employees were at the park.

"Not enough," said Derek. "Haven't been able to reach him by phone. I'll keep trying. I think he has about six landscapers and carpenters there today. He's got a guy who runs the backhoe and dozer, and a gravel truck for transporting the big animals occasionally."

"He transports animals in a gravel truck?" Kyle asked.

"Long story, Lansdowne. But when you see one of those buffalo, pray he doesn't see you first if you're on the same side of the fence."

After nearly hitting three deer who were disoriented in the smoke, Derek gripped the steering wheel and turned on the window cleaner and wiper blades, which gummed up into thick grey mud.

"Dammit."

One of the men rolled down the passenger window and poured water over the glass, sending dirty smoke-filled drops inside the cab. But it worked and soon Derek could speed up a little with better visibility.

They were driving through one of the tallest redwood forests in the county, but not a single tree was visible. He watched the old camp sign move past them, and he hit the brakes. He backed up slowly.

"Watch out back for me. The rear camera isn't working."

"Roger that," one of the men said.

The park sign was at it's usual cocky angle, but what alarmed Derek the most was that the top of the sign was actually burning.

He stopped in front of the metal gates and stuck his arm into the thick smokey air, pushing the intercom key, waiting for a response.

"Yo, Derek, that you?"

"Yessir. And I brought some friends. You gonna let us in? The gate working?"

"Thank God. Well, let's give this old gate a try."

Slowly, the large sides opened, the metal screeching like it was about to fail. Derek got out and forced the gate closed, upset with himself for not bringing his keys and clicker.

His phone buzzed, and he heard Gerson bark orders he couldn't understand.

"Anyone catch that?"

"Said something like 'they're out'."

"Fuck!" Derek pounded on his steering wheel, grabbed the phone, and yelled into it, "Where do we go? Where are you?"

"I'm with the guests. We got a Girl Scout Troupe of ten year olds. Meet me at the lodge, but you hear the stampede, you head for the bushes, hear?"

"Fuck me," whispered Fredo.

Of course there would be a troupe of Girl Scouts, Derek mused, grinding his teeth. What else could go wrong?

Just then, they were confronted with several black and white shapes, two of which seemed to leap over the truck. A third one didn't quite make the hurdle and collapsed on the hood of the formerly white truck, dusty hooves and legs scrambled in amber colored liquid, trying to get traction, before sliding off to the side. They watched the animal run into the thick jungle brush without so much as a whimper.

"Zebra. We just got run over by a herd of zebra," said Fredo.

"Not something you see every day, now, do you?" the tall medic said. He was the calmest one in the truck.

"They running away from the fire?" Kyle asked. "Or just running?"

But Derek didn't have to explain. They all felt the lumbering ground shake like a train was coming straight for them.

"Hold on," shouted Derek as he made a hard right into the brush, aimed down a small embankment and through a shallow creek bed up to the other side, and stopped.

The train got louder until the thunderous demonstration of angry or scared Cape Buffalo stormed past them on their way to an encounter with a fence somewhere. "The fencing will hold them, but they'll be pissed as hell."

"They were chasing the zebras?" someone asked.

"Not exactly. Everyone gets out of their way. Unless you have a .416 with a tranq cartridge."

The thunder had subsided such that they could even hear the water from the creek. Derek feathered the gas, on the lookout for something else that might ram the truck. He figured he'd voided his contract by now, but it would be a story that could be fun to tell, if he survived.

The lodge was lit by noisy generators, and the smoke was somewhat dissipated by huge circular blowers he'd seen in the vineyards before. That meant the power was gone, which might affect some of the gates, Derek worried.

A single large screen TV was showing the news reports, and a band of young girls with masks on their faces sat in orderly fashion with their two college-aged scout leaders. Horace was unlocking a metal cabinet nearby and removing the safety chain. He brought out an assortment of hunting rifles but strapped to his back was his beloved Remington.

He surveyed the group of SEALs before him.

"Thank you for your help. I can sure use it. Half my guys have fled, and those sons of bitches took my trucks and most my ATVs too."

"They take the dozer?" Derek asked.

"No, I think that was determined to be too slow. I still have my gravel truck too. But I'm short the Land Rovers and the Toros."

"What's the plan?" asked Kyle.

"Stay alive. Get these girls home safe. Try not to lose too many animals."

"So, what do you need first?" Kyle asked again.

"Mind if I ask you boys to make some sandwiches? They've devoured their day packs and haven't had a meal in about ten hours. I got bread and fixings in the kitchen. Derek can show you."

He led them to the two walk-in refrigerators, filled with baskets of fruit, crates of milk, sodas and lots of water. They made an assembly line and returned to the hall with more than two dozen sandwiches displayed on a large cooking sheet. The girls surrounded them and stuffed their pockets with chips while devouring the sandwiches.

Gerson sat with the men, and whispered out of earshot of the Girl Scouts. "We got two problems. My fences are mostly metal, but I got some wood here and there. Now, metal melts if it gets hot enough, and that fire is going to sideswipe us, according to the NIXLE reports."

"There's the wind too. They're worried about St. Helena," added Derek.

"I'm sorry to say that coming this way will save St. Helena. But if it goes that way, it will burn the town down, and then come for us. No, gents. I think we need a miracle."

"So we're to protect the fences?"

"That's our only defense. And all I got are firehoses and two pumps. My lake is down right now and full of muck, but that's the best water supply we got. If you guys can keep those fences from burning, I think these animals will survive the smoke and will be all right. So, wear your masks."

"You got anything we can put into the gravel truck?" asked Kyle?

"Not following."

"You got any water tanks?"

"I have one. Just one. But I got some barrels of cooking oil and some weed killer. Nasty stuff."

"I think that's flammable. But let's use the cooking oil. Where do we dump it?" asked Derek.

Gerson lit up like a Christmas Tree. "I got just the spot. You roll that stuff—it will take two of you—downhill to the back gate. Behind there is a regular racetrack for the Buffalo. You dump it there. A few of them will be surprised and stumble. But that could slow them down. We need to keep them calm, or they'll tear up everything."

"What about blowing the oil on them direct?"

"Oh, that oil will be all over them, trust me. They'll do all the lathering needed."

Horace shook his head, laughing, and walked down the hallway get the doses of tranq. He brought a couple of the men with him to help him collect the water tanks, and the two pieces of heavy equipment. He addressed them before moving on.

"We'll be back in about twenty. Take a quick catnap so you're fresh. Probably will be the last chance you have to sleep for awhile."

They watched him waddle away.

Derek looked at the guys who were used to emergencies. Nothing compared to this. Their enemy was Mother Nature and, for some reason, she wanted to punish Napa and Sonoma Counties and all the people and animals who lived there.

"If it looks like a lost cause," Derek started, "we bundle up the girls in wet blankets and make a run for it in that gravel truck. I'll go ahead with the dozer, cutting a path. But it would be nice if we didn't have to bust out of here. Those animals would be all over the valley floor."

"That would be a picture, wouldn't it?" said Fredo. "Zebras grazing on grapes and big cats chasing goats and sheep in the tasting rooms."

The chuckle that followed helped everybody. They were made for things like this even though they'd never fought a fire like this one.

The tall SEAL medic pointed a banana at Derek. "When we're all done and if it survives, we all get free passes to bring the kids, right?"

"Deal," Derek said fist-bumping him in return.

CHAPTER 22

REMY DROVE STRAIGHT through to Calistoga and was stopped at the road closure. The reports she'd been listening to all night long were devastating. Some two hundred homes had been lost so far, and it was confirmed that nearly thirty people had lost their lives. The fire was only about five percent contained.

Her grandfather had been evacuated and was staying in a hotel down in the Bay Area, along with residents from several other facilities. They evacuated two hospitals, sending patients to Sacramento or San Francisco. Some were even flown out of state.

St. Helena was a ghost town. Volunteers watched for stray pets that ran away in the confusion, running to capture them, giving them a good hug and a decent meal away from the smoke. But Remy was going nuts waiting.

She dialed Derek's number and was surprised he picked up. His voice was cool and flat.

"I know you're busy, Derek. Do you need anything?"

"As in you're going to get it to us how?"

"I know some back roads my grandfather taught me. What would you like if you could have anything at all?"

"A water truck."

"A water truck. Okay, let's hear your second choice."

"Wait a minute, you're up here?"

"I am."

"I told you to stay back down in Coronado."

"And I didn't listen to you. Are you surprised?"

He paused. His answer, *no,* was a little weak.

"Tell me how I can help you."

"I don't want you to get involved. We got a whole lot of wild animals, and a fuckin' Girl Scout troupe stranded here. Trying to keep the two separated is going to be a tall order. But we need to keep the fences from burning or melting."

"You have power?"

"Yes, propane. I think we have enough for several days. We'll probably run out of drinking water in a couple, but we have lots of other stuff."

"Blankets?" she asked.

"All the girls are huddled in the center lobby. We have enough to keep them warm."

"How about enough to keep them from getting burned, or are you sure you can wait it out?"

"Okay, blankets. But have someone else bring them in."

"Like who? Name somebody."

"Remy, quit being so stubborn. It's too dangerous."

"You have anyone minding the girls?"

"Yes, they have two counselors, guides or whatever they're called."

"So we're back to the water truck."

"Afraid so."

"The Red Cross is handing out some blankets. Maybe I can snag a few for you, but they're flimsy. I can get some waters."

"Don't."

"How about you let me decide if I can do it first. Then you can decide if you want the help, Derek. That fair?"

He wasn't going to stop trying to talk her out of it so she hung up on him. That would deliver the message that she was serious.

Her next call was to Knudsen.

"How's the winery?"

"Lots of damage, but I think we're going to be okay. The wind is shifting, which isn't good news for St. Helena."

"Yes, I know. Just talked to Derek."

"He said he was going to the camp. We're fine."

"I got a favor to ask. You happen to have any water trucks over there at the winery?"

"Nope. They contract that out when they're working the field."

"Do you know how I could get one?"

"Remy, water trucks would be in huge demand right now. Even if I had one, they'd stop me and confiscate it. It's like a war zone down there."

"I know. That's where I'm calling from. Derek and the park need water to keep the fences from burning."

"Gosh, I don't even know if I could fill up the wine transport from the Jackson's well. It would likely take me two days to fill those tankers."

"They're tankers?"

"Yes, steel tankers. Filled with wine."

"Filled with wine. How many do you have?"

"I'm looking at two. It would take about two hours to empty the thing, and by the time we filled them up, it would probably be too late."

"But what if you don't empty them?"

"But they're filled with wine."

"Are they flammable?"

"No, wine doesn't have enough alcohol to be flammable. But they're headed to the central valley to be stored in barrels there."

"You have hoses?"

"Sure."

"Can you drive one?"

"Wait a minute, Remy, you're not saying I should drive a transport filled with wine and dump it on the fencing at the park are you?"

"No, I'm saying you could drive one and I could drive the other."

"That's not a good idea. Besides, that wine is already sold."

"So why don't I make a higher offer?"

"Nobody does that."

"Nobody has had to save ten little Girl Scouts and a band of SEALs trying to save some rare and exotic animals. It would be a shame to see everything go up in smoke just because no one agreed to buy that wine and deliver it in time to help out. Wouldn't it?"

"I'll have to ask the Jacksons."

"I'll pay their price. I have an inheritance. I can't think of anything I'd rather invest in. You willing to take a risk with me?"

"You're bonkers, Remy."

"No, Knudsen. I'm a woman obsessed with getting her way. And I want to help Derek and the other SEALs save the day."

"I can't believe I'm going to do this."

Remy smiled. "Knudsen, you were always a much better friend than Ray ever was. You're the reason we got back together. Now you gotta help us keep it that way. Go find the keys, both sets."

Remy texted directions to the Jackson Winery on her phone, and because the main roads were blocked off, she entered from the service entrance that all the crews and large equipment used. She thought that would probably be where the large tankers would be.

An older gentleman was standing by Derek, and her stomach did a double flop to the floorboards.

She got out of the Hummer and extended her hand. The gentleman didn't take it, but stared into her eyes as he chewed on a toothpick.

She extended her hand again. "I'm Remington Bolt."

"You Harrison Bolt's granddaughter?"

"Yessir. You know my grandfather?"

"I do." His deadpan expression didn't give any of his inner feelings away. Remy wasn't sure her plan was going to work, all of a sudden. They could have some history, and that history could be either good or bad.

"And that would mean that your grandmother would have been Una," he whispered, a slight hitch to his voice.

"Yes, she was my grandmother, though I didn't know her well. I was little."

"I loved your grandmother nearly more than I loved myself back in those days. But your grandfather had all the charm. He was a fast-talking dreamer of a man, and she had no right to go off with him. I could have given her all of this," he said as he swung his arm in an arc, showing the beautiful vineyards.

Remy quickly checked on Knudsen, who gave her a very slight shrug to say he had no clue which way this was going to go.

"Sir, I'm afraid all this—"

"You have two minutes for this old man to tell you a thing or two. I see a bit of her in you. But with this scheme to steal my wine and use it to save a God-damned zoo and some crazy-assed peg-legged washed up military hero—that's coming straight from your grandfather's side. I see a whole lot of Harrison Bolt in that plan."

"He knows nothing about this."

"Of course he doesn't. He doesn't know how to execute. He just dreams. Crashes cars and dreams."

"And I love him for his dreams. Just like you loved Una for her heart. It was her decision, wasn't it?"

"It was."

"And you let her go with him."

"It was the biggest regret of my life."

"Sir, I'm going to pay you for this wine. Do you want to know where the money is going to come from? It's from the money she left me when she passed. It's Una's money that you'll have. As much as it takes."

He stood up, bending back and taking another long look at her from a slight distance. Then he nodded.

"Is there a love story there?"

"Yes, there most definitely is. The love of my life is depending on me bringing something that will keep him and his SEAL buddies safe and save all the animals *and* a small troupe of Girl Scouts who happened to pick this weekend for an adventure."

"Take the wine. When you get done with all this, if you need a position in sales and marketing, I have a good spot for you. No one has ever talked me out of my wine before."

Knudsen practically stepped on his lower lip. "Thank you so much, sir."

They felt the warm wind and saw a new burst of flames at the top of the hill.

"Better hurry, Remington Bolt. Your destiny awaits."

CHAPTER 23

THE MEN USED propane-fired water pumps to flush contents from the lagoon. Heavy Duct Tape was used to string the sanitary hoses together, working in shifts of two all night long, so they could access the water without clearing a path through the jungle. Gerson's gravel truck held the green water tank the swampy water was pumped into. Several times they ran across vegetation tangles and, once, a fish that temporarily clogged the operation and split the taping, sending water spraying over everyone. It was actually kind of pleasant when that happened, Derek thought. Even though it was past midnight, with all the smoke and flames in the valley, it was hot and muggy, and the ash stuck to everything.

The air had gotten so foul that, even with the masks, their lungs were filling with soot, so they took turns with twenty minute intervals inside the gravel truck's cab. That left the other four men to get an hour of sleep before their shift.

After loading up and storing the equipment and hoses to keep from getting trampled, they headed for the perimeter fencing.

The main gate was where the bulk of the wooden fences were built, but that was also farther away from the fire and not as much at risk. Oddly enough, it had been a design requirement that they use local special treated and naturally stained redwood when the camp got its operating permits. The entrance was secure for now, but only if its sides remained intact. And only if they could keep it wet.

Those who couldn't fit into the cab rode in back and helped to balance the huge tank as they stopped at the various stops along the outside wall. It took about ten minutes to lumber through the crisscross of stampede trails and gravel roads to make it to each of the planned stops. Gerson reminded them that this would have to be repeated at regular intervals through-out the next twenty-four hours, when they would know more about the condition of the fire containment.

Derek and Gerson were spraying down the fencing while the hoses were draped and held in position by other hands. A fire hose bib was placed on the end which served as an on/off switch, but also gave the area a wide spray.

They took turns holding the end, since the water

pressure made it nearly unmanageable. All the surrounding ground nearly twenty feet in diameter was also soaked, including redwoods and other vegetation planted along the fenceline.

After several moments, they turned off the pumps and stopped to listen when they began to feel the rumble of a stampede approaching. So far, they'd not had an appearance from the buffalo.

"I think they don't like the sound of the pumps."

"What do we do if they show up?" asked Derek.

"We spray them. They're not afraid of the water, of course, but they don't like it in their faces, and I'm thinking they'll turn," Horace shouted in answer.

"Gotcha."

Several large cats ran into the clearing and then disappeared just as quickly. There were several curious monkeys and some local deer, all very tentative and brief in their appearance.

Finally, they had completed the perimeter soak and came upon the main gate for their last stretch. Water was getting low, which meant the whole process would have to be repeated all over again. But since they had driven nearly the entire perimeter, the men relaxed a bit, feeling confident they'd protected the camp in the event it came too close or breached the fencing. But everyone knew if that wind kept picking up, it could just blow a torch right through the middle of the camp, especially come nightfall when the wind blew stronger. That would mean disaster.

Gerson had cleared more of the brush inside the gate and had done the same outside, but the long winding trail getting there was grossly overhung with scrub oaks, madrone, and some tall pine and fir trees, making any impending rescue operation difficult. The forest floor was also filled with dead or rotting branches that had accumulated over the years.

They turned on the pumps and discovered they were nearly out of propane. Without an ATV, they'd have to take the whole truck back to the center for new supplies.

"Let's run 'er out and then we'll leave it be for now. Take a rest, check on the girls and then get something to eat. How does that sound?" yelled Gerson.

"Right by me," said Kyle. Most the group agreed.

The water began to sputter as each pump shut off.

"I say we dump the rest of water on the ground here," suggested Derek. "It will be mucky in a passenger car, but will also slow down the buffalo."

"Good idea," said Horace.

The men rolled the water tank on its side, and poured the green liquid all over the clearing just inside the entrance. There had not been much left, but it was better than hauling it back and forth again.

As they were getting ready to leave, they felt a low

vibration. Something large was headed toward them, getting closer. It didn't come from inside the camp. It came from the forest outside.

Derek thought perhaps it was a fire truck or some rescue operation, but was disappointed when he recognized a big green wine tanker truck, with another right behind it. What was even more strange was that Remy was behind the wheel of the second one.

They stopped just outside, and Knudsen jumped from the cab of the first one. "Hey, someone order some wine?" he shouted.

He was greeted with cheers and whistles.

"I'll be damned," whispered Gerson. "If that fire gets too close, I'll just drown myself in that big old vat and die a happy man!" He ran for the control box and punched in the code. "You get those puppies in here quickly."

Derek had broken through the opening as soon as the gate began to move, pulled open the driver door of the second tanker and jerked Remy out. She tore herself loose and looked defiantly back at him, her jaw tight.

"What the hell are you doing here?" he asked, looking at her dirt-smudged face and sweaty chest. "You shouldn't be here. It's too dangerous."

Remy placed her hands on her hips, shouting back. "You said you wanted water tanker trucks. Well, I couldn't get the water, but I got something that will work just the same."

She tossed him the keys and made her way to greet the others.

Derek climbed into the cab, started the engine, and followed Knudsen inside. After parking, he left the tanker running while Kyle and Gerson closed the gate behind him.

"Okay, I'd say it's time to go get some food, get cleaned up, and check on the kids. These two angels have saved us from having to spend all night filling up our water tank." He bowed to Remy. "But in the morning, we're gonna have to replenish our supply. No telling what may befall us."

"We need to check with CalFire and let them know we're here," said Kyle.

"Good idea. You do that. Don't let them tell you it's a mandatory evacuation. We got the animals to protect."

Remy was surrounded by the other Team guys, shaking hands and getting hugs and pats on the back. Of course, Knudsen was as well, but Derek was only interested in Remy at the moment. So much had happened, he had to think about it before he remembered why he'd been so upset with her. He shelved it and stuffed it in the back of his brain for later.

She rode with Gerson and Kyle up front in the

gravel truck. Fredo rode with him. The four others rode with Knudsen, or in the back. They started the slow caravan back to the lodge.

The girls had made a mess of the kitchen, leaving chocolate and melted marshmallows on the stove, partially burned. They were all glued to a movie on the big screen. Gerson was furious at the condition of his kitchen.

"Little asswipes," he muttered under his breath.

Remy walked around the tall structure, looking at all the pictures of celebrities who had stayed there. When she saw Gerson's reaction, she got after the girls, coming down hardest on their teen advisors.

"We're working hard to make this as safe as possible, but you guys have to help out." She shook her head at the older girls. "This isn't responsible. These guys have been working nearly all night and day. It would have been nice to come home to a good meal, but instead they find that you've been making S'Mores. Do you realize how critical this is?"

She started cleaning up, so Derek began to help.

"Well, since we're the only cooks, I guess it's on us to make dinner," he said.

Remy barely looked at him. "You go take a shower. No telling how much fresh water we'll have when that lot gets ready for bed. I'll start something and then we can trade, deal?"

He threw down his towel and agreed, taking the stairs two at a time.

He had just one clean set of clothes left, and was tempted to ask the girls to do some laundry, but didn't want to waste water. Kyle walked in the bathroom reading his cell.

"It's not looking good tonight. Fire's only about ten miles away, dammit. If we get a big gust, it can easily go more than five miles an hour. Remember how it jumped the freeway?"

"What did CalFire say?"

"Busy signal. I can only imagine how someone stranded out in these woods with the fire heading straight for them would feel. But damn, I don't hear a single rescue helicopter going, so you?"

"Nope. Do they say anything about it?"

"There's a local AM radio station who's been doing good work broadcasting names of people missing, or found, or what people can do with a stray or lost pet. They've been interviewing the Sheriff and people from CDC. It's bad, Derek. Really bad."

"You tell them about our location?"

"Sure did. Turns out Gerson is some kind of eccentric hero. They were all over that. Want to do an interview later by phone."

"Don't tell them about me. They'll be wanting to do a campfire cooking show," laughed Derek.

Derek felt better being clean. Gerson gathered their things and said they could spare one wash load, but after that, they'd be showering and washing in wine. It didn't seem like such a bad idea.

Fredo and a couple of the other guys had siphoned off some of the wine and placed it on the table. Gerson found some Jack Daniels and a few six packs of beer, and then discovered the scouts had gotten into his stash of water.

"Okay, girls," he said as he ran into the room with two half-empty water bottles. "This is not okay. We have a limited amount of this stuff, which might be what will keep you alive." He walked over to the teens, grabbing them by the shirt collar. "You two are responsible. Everything is rationed. If I say they can't eat it, they don't, get it? If you think I'm going to be happy getting phone calls asking if they can have popcorn or peanut butter and jelly, you're crazy. Now, get in there and clean up that storage locker. Put all the water in one container. We don't waste a drop, okay?"

"Yessir," they said in unison. The Girl Scouts turned off the movie and sat on the couches and chairs in the grand room.

"I think a few of you can go help Remy in the kitchen. The rest of you are going to do garbage detail and cleanup. This isn't a party. This is survival," he shouted.

Little footsteps ran to the kitchen where Remy was making a large pot of vegetable stew. Derek joined them.

"Smells great. What can I do?"

"That water he put back in the storage? Go get that and I'm going to boil noodles."

He did as he was asked, placing the water in a large pot and adding some tap water. "Hey, Gerson," he said over his shoulder. "How deep is the well?"

"Deep enough. But it's a solar well, and we used the storage tank we normally would have hooked up to it. But our water's good. Just not at night."

"I can rig a generator to it, if you like," said one of the SEALs.

"There we go. Problem solved," mused Derek as he turned on the commercial stove and covered the pot. He leaned over Remy's shoulder, placing his chin there.

"I'd take you camping any day. You learn this at CCA?"

"My grandmother's recipe. Was grandpa's favorite. First thing I learned to cook."

She walked into the pantry and held up two brownie boxes, shaking them in Gerson's direction. Without saying a word, she pointed to the girls. He gave her the nod of approval.

"After dinner, girls, and after we clean up, you're

going to make some brownies. How is that?"

She was surrounded by several of the girls and handed them the garlic bread she'd warmed, paper plates and plastic utensils.

"Now go set the table," she said, directing them to the long half-log redwood table in the middle of the room. As the last SEAL made it downstairs, the simple dinner was prepared and being served up.

THE FIRE HAD switched course and was actually climbing the hills on the other side of the valley, which is where resources had been diverted. The updates were looking more and more promising.

"We're not out of danger yet. But I think we can all get some rest, if we take turns."

Gerson gave the men their choice of sleeping inside, or outside in the glamping tents, minus the heated mattresses. He asked for a couple of them to stay inside watching the news and guarding the girls. Like the night before, they were to take four-hour shifts.

"You get some rest, Gerson. We'll take your shift," said Kyle.

"I'm grateful for that kindness. I'm going to take you up on that." He left.

"Can I show you to your tent, Miss?" asked Derek when they were left alone.

He could see she was softening, but she still put up

a little resistance. "I'm still waiting for my thank you."

Derek was embarrassed. "You're right. But my first reaction was for your safety. Half that forest is on fire, and you came through there."

"I knew that road and I checked the maps they have posted everywhere. We weren't anywhere near the fire."

They started down the steps to the camping area. He took her hand, and she didn't pull away. "Thank you for being brilliant, Remy, for thinking out of the box. I just didn't want you hurt. That's all I meant."

"I know it."

They found a tent with a view of the center. Shaking all the embers and ash from the white canvas with poles on the inside, they re-zipped the flap opening and undressed for bed.

The king mattress felt like a cloud. He lay back, watched Remy crawl in beside him, and could not keep his eyes open, even for her. The last he remembered was her little smirk and the feel of the small of her back as she nudged close to him.

CHAPTER 24

REMY WOKE UP to the sounds of screaming. At first, she didn't know where she was and thought she'd had a bad dream, but as her eyes adjusted, her first deep inhale threw her into a coughing fit. Derek was up and dressed in a flash. The sky was glowing red all around them, and the smoke was twice as thick as before.

"Something's changed. We gotta get out of here," he said. Remy checked her watch and discovered it was four-thirty in the morning.

They ran to the lodge, finding the girls in their pajamas, and Kyle glued to his cell.

"Fire's combined, jumped the ridge and is coming back this way. I'm told we have to evacuate."

"I'm not leaving," barked Gerson. "I can't leave my animals. "But, God damn it, one of you have to get the girls out. Take the gravel truck."

"I don't think it's safe," Derek said.

Kyle put his finger in the air and played a broadcast from the AM station in Santa Rosa.

…updates on road closures as we get them. Next update in fifteen minutes. Folks, these are coming in fast and furious, so not all of them are here. But everything south of Calistoga Road is in flames. We're expecting total losses there. It's mainly rural…

"Fuck! That's us," shouted Gerson.

Remy and Derek stared at each other. Fredo and several others on the Team tried their cell phones and not getting through.

…Mr. Gerson is a friend of the show, and if you can hear this broadcast, sir, please confirm that your position is safe at this time. Our efforts to contact you have been unsuccessful….

…Yes, Mr. Gerson's employee, Kyle, called us earlier and all was well. The smoke had thinned and they were hoping to be out of harm's way. Please call back if you hear this message, or anyone who knows about Wet N Wild animal park in St. Helena.

"My cell is dead. How'd you get reception, Kyle?" Gerson asked.

"Different cell tower. I'm connected to a SAT linkup, and none of you are supposed to know that."

"So, if the towers burn, there's no reception."

"Yup," Kyle said.

"Wonder how many people have their cell phone as

their emergency number?" asked Fredo.

Remy shuddered.

"So I'm going to call them and ask for help." Kyle turned off the broadcast and routed his call out number then dialed the radio station like he'd done before. "This is Kyle at Wet N Wild for Alice Corwin."

He made the message short and sweet. Told them what they were doing, and then put Gerson on the line with a slightly different style. He told the audience of over five hundred thousand listeners that, no matter how bad it got, he was staying with his animals, and if they wanted him to evacuate, they'd have to bring in the National Guard and haul him out. As the producer asked more questions he hung up.

Everyone's jaw dropped.

"Look, we don't have time for this. I say we get working on the perimeter. That will tell us what's going on. Our NIXLE won't work now, unless you can get it, Kyle?"

"Flying blind here," he answered. "I think that's a good move. You girls are going to have to behave. Stay here. If fire breaches the fencing, one of the trucks will come get you, and we'll have to fight our way out. So be ready. Keep your clothes, shoes and socks on, and be ready if we need to evacuate."

Gerson walked into the room with three Remingtons and loaded them up with tranq cartridges. He put his hand on several other boxes. "I don't want to have to euthanize my animals, but we have to bring these in case the very worst happens. And I'll use it if one of you gets in trouble. But until then, I'm issuing two tranq cartridges per rifle. If you aim right, one will stop the buffalo. None of the other animals can handle this dose. Only if you have to, send the second one. And then you know what to do after that, if you have to."

He handed Kyle the first one then Derek the second.

"And for fuck's sake, don't miss. These fuckers cost me a hundred bucks a piece!"

Remy was shocked.

"We have to have a driver, two handlers, and a shooter on each of the two tanker trucks," continued Gerson.

Remy was surprised when Derek handed his rifle to her. Gerson looked at him like he was crazy. "What you doin', Derek? No time for fuckin' games."

"She can't do the heavy lifting. She can drive, yet I know the terrain better. But she sure as hell can shoot. We're in good hands."

Remy took the canvas ammo bag, strapped the rifle to her back, and didn't look anyone in the eye, heading for the trucks. It was important not to show weakness or a lack of confidence. Time to think about all that was *after* the event, not before. Her grandfather had taught her that.

Derek drove, and she sat next to him while they got the tanker in place. They were headed in the direction of the rosy glow, which was not an early morning sunrise. The whole ridge was on fire. They didn't waste time on *thanks for the vote of confidence* or *I believe in* you stuff. They didn't say anything at all. Remy knew he was as scared as she was.

She discovered the source of the screaming that had awakened her. It had been monkeys who were trumpeting each other to leave the area. The electric fencing still held, and they would not go anywhere near it, unless an opening developed. They knew they were trapped, but they'd rather burn than cross those fences. Remy's heart sank.

Large grey chards of light fell from the sky as the bright orange sun rose. They could easily see the flames through the trees, which had now gotten sparse as the fire advanced. When they reached the outside boundary line, they were relieved to note the vegetation was still intact, and the fence was not trampled or busted open.

The men placed the hose in place, rigged the opening so it wouldn't leak, and turned the truck's pump on. Gallons of the deep red liquid sprayed in the air, coating trees and shrubs while sending animals off in the opposite direction and covering the fencing and beyond.

Remy had climbed up the ladder at the back of the tanker and sat, perched above it all, to watch for signs of anything coming their way. The flames in the distance were enormous, looking to be several stories high and, though several miles away still, starting to scorch her face. One of the men gave her a wet bandana, soaked in wine. She tied it over her nose and mouth, keeping her skin cool, preferring to use it rather than the masks Gerson had issued them.

They crawled at a snail's pace for the next two hours, following the fencing, while the contents of the tanker were released. The other tanker had moved in the opposite direction and now was coming into view. It was good news. That meant that the perimeter had not been broken and that for now, everything in the park was safe.

They returned to the place where the water had been dumped. The tanker spun out briefly then made it halfway to the other side before the double rear axle sank in the ground. Derek swore a blue streak as he tried to back up slowly, and then go forward, but the wheels were getting mired deeper and deeper. The size of the vehicle made it impossible to find something large enough to use as a wedge.

And then the rumbling started. Remy knew exactly what it was, because it wasn't like anything she'd ever felt or seen before. A herd of very angry Cape Buffalo was cresting over a small swale, one smaller buffalo leading the pack. But behind loomed the largest animal she'd ever seen.

She readied her rifle and heard Kyle and Gerson ready theirs. Looking at the dust and soot cloud, she knew if she could get a clear angle, the right choice would be to wound or hit the smaller buffalo in front, which might cause a chain reaction and stop the rest. But as she squinted and examined the herd further, she noticed that between the legs of the smaller animal was a calf, running for its life, being nudged by the beast behind it.

Intuition told her this was mother and child. She took aim at the large male with the red eyes, now threatening to overrun the little family unit and was about to pull the trigger when the thunderous vibration caused her foot to slip. She fell to the ground. She had just enough time to kneel, take aim, and fire the .416 Magnum round from her lower vantage point, hitting the beast in the neck below his ear. The recoil sent her back on her butt nearly two feet, but she didn't take her eyes off the oncoming herd.

The large male collapsed and tumbled over the female, who had been hit with someone else's round. The calf ran straight for the tanker truck, hit the steel shell, and slid into the undercarriage, scratching and screaming.

She couldn't take her eyes off the male, whose one visible red eye fluttered and then rolled back. Both animals slid several feet in the mud. The rest of the herd stumbled, got up awkwardly, and redirected, soon leaving the scene. Dirt and large rocks were flying, falling all around the two dark shapes in front of her. Something hit her from the side, and it surprised her. She focused on the cow's face until her red eye closed.

That was the last thing she remembered before everything went black.

CHAPTER 25

D EREK THOUGHT HE'D lost Remy that night. Without a rifle, because he had given Remy the one he was supposed to use, he was powerless to stop the stampeding horde from wiping her off the face of the earth. And although Kyle and Gerson both fired shots, it was Remy who had saved herself. In the face of danger, she remained calm, reaching out well beyond what she'd ever done before and created a miracle.

Remy was that miracle to him. He'd come so close to losing her twice by his own misunderstanding and stupid behavior. How could he have been so blind to not understand the joy and life she brought to everything she touched? He was the lucky recipient of her love, whether or not he accepted it.

True to form, when she came to, lying on the muddy ground that night, fire all around them, smoke making everyone choke, the first thing she asked about was the calf. That silly scared little thing was still trying to extricate herself from the undercarriage of that damned wine tanker until two SEALs climbed underneath and gently removed her and untangled her broken leg.

Gerson said he was going to name her Remington. She was casted by a vet flown in from a South African game preserve, all paid for by a private benefactor, and would spend some time with her mother in a private pen Gerson was going to construct, now that his work crew had returned.

The fire also claimed part of the culinary school. A late night frantic call to Gerson from a panicked Miss Bernstein was patched through by the Sheriff to the CDC, and Horace was off to save her, though nearly stopped at several barricades. But after getting her to the emergency shelter, he was right back at his camp, tending to the animals and re-checking his perimeter systems.

The fire came very close to the camp that night, but not a single animal perished. As soon as it re-opened and word flew across the news wires what had happened there, bookings flooded in. Gerson was going to get all the help he needed. He was enjoying all the interviews, and his picture was even plastered on the cover of National Geographic Magazine. He'd told Derek that he'd have preferred GQ, but he wasn't quibbling.

Kyle and the rest of SEAL Team 3, and a couple of guys from Team 5 returned to Coronado after helping with the cleanup and return of the tankers.

The culinary school was also flooded with applications. The TV series was altered and re-named Glampout Cookout. Derek got his wish to make Remy the co-star. There would be no more babes in skimpy clothes trying to embarrass him, or themselves.

CCA awarded Gerson a proclamation and medal, which he wore every day thereafter. Derek learned Horace was seen at the Admin building more and more as the days passed.

The school named a veteran's program after Derek, called the Faraway Veterans Scholarship. Part of the tuition was predicated on the student working ten hours a week at Gerson's camp, just like Derek had done.

But Remy was the real star. And she didn't even want it. It took her grandfather to talk her into going on with him. The final straw had been that they offered to film the show at Jackson's winery, and Mr. Jackson was included, because of his generosity in donating the wine that perhaps helped save the day.

She told Derek the story about her grandmother, and they decided never to tell old Harrison Bolt, who continued driving his Shelby through St. Helena, impressing all the older ladies, until he was pulled over by Connor Jackson himself. At court, his license was pulled. It was a bittersweet ending to a passion of his. He refused to get rid of the car, so it sat in the VIP visitor's spot at the retirement home he bought into.

They went back to school, and now people stopped them both. She sat for interviews at his side, as it should have always been.

The weeks flew by, and at last, they'd scheduled the filming date. It was her time to be hesitant. She seemed to finally have accepted her fate, though she'd tried to talk him out of it nearly every day the last week. He could tell nervousness was looming large—so large that he refused to let her drive several days before their filming.

Remy's big debut was today. He knew it would be a day neither one of them would forget.

He held her hand under the countertop as they stood together in their white jackets bracing against the bright lights and heat of the equipment. Jackson's winery kitchen had just undergone a remodel with brand new equipment never used before. He knew none of that mattered to her, though. She'd told him it felt more like a firing squad than an episode recorded for entertainment.

He'd had the devilish idea to do something simple, so he chose to decorate a cake with chocolate frosting. He began by explaining all the different origins of chocolate and how it was one of the most sought after ingredients in the history of the world. How wars had been fought and fortunes lost over chocolate.

The students in his class had given them a specially prepared dark fudge cake to use in the demonstration.

She stood by his side as he smeared his half-cup of butter into the deep stainless steel bowl with a bright red spatula. Then he added powdered sugar, some vanilla, condensed milk and a little hot water. Last came the unsweetened cocoa and a little more hot water until it was the desired consistency. Remy followed suit, while he watched her. He noticed her hand was shaking and he held it steady at one point, just so she knew he was there and not to be afraid.

Then Derek demonstrated all the other flavorings that could be added to enhance the basic chocolate frosting as he whipped the creamy dark substance until it was completely blended smooth. He turned to watch Remy mirror him, just a few steps behind.

"Now we taste it," he said to the camera. For the benefit of repeat viewers, he wiggled his eyebrows and showed off his conspiratorial smile. He rolled a big dollop of the mixture on the end of his spatula and held it out for her tongue. Of course, he slightly missed, on purpose. Reflexively, Remy brought her hands up to her face to wipe away the excess, and his hand gripped her wrist, stopping her.

Looking back at the camera, he threw out another devilish grin, bent down and licked the chocolate from her upper lip and cheek and the tip of her nose.

Remy couldn't stop giggling. The crew was laughing.

He beckoned to her to do the same for him. Remy took great pains, even biting her lower lip, to lather the chocolate across his lips and then touched him under the counter while her tongue and mouth sucked the sweetness from him. Instead of being repelled, Derek pushed his pelvis into Remy's hand and her blush was astonishing and caught on camera.

"Now for the decoration," he said into the camera. Pulling the cake toward him, he handed Remy his spatula and invited her to cover the top with her own frosting.

Her fluid motions stalled when her spatula ran across something sharp—something with a rounded edge embedded into the devils food cake itself. She immediately stared up at him in alarm, whispering.

"We've got something here, Derek. I think we have a—"

"Humor me," he said as he stepped behind her, placed his hand over hers and smoothed the chocolate in tandem motions. Still clutching over her hand, he maneuvered the spatula into the cake and lifted the object out.

He knew what it was, the camera crew knew what it was, the CCA class, watching it live, knew what it was, but he wanted to see it in her eyes. He showed her the new ring. This one was bigger. And this one would fit, he was sure. Her eyes watered and she brushed his cheek with her own, smearing more chocolate between them, which didn't matter to him at all.

He slid the ring with the chocolate still covering both their hands, and delighted in seeing that it easily seated home, where he vowed it would always stay.

John McCormick tossed his head from side to side off camera, frowning, unimpressed. But all the women on the crew let out sighs and Derek even heard someone whisper, "Oh, that was so nice."

Jackson told the audience that he'd be honored to host the wedding at his winery. He and Derek had already set the date.

"The students at CCA and my future daughter-in-law, Chloe, are all in on it and going to cater for you. It's all been arranged," said the old man.

She scanned the film crew, the vineyard, the chocolate mess and the half-frosted cake before her, held out her ring and smiled at Mr. Jackson. She turned to Derek. "I can't believe it. You did all this? Where did you learn to—?"

"Welcome to my show, Remy. The first of many."

ABOUT THE AUTHOR

 NYT and USA Today best-selling author Sharon Hamilton's award-winning Navy SEAL Brotherhood series have been a fan favorite from the day the first one was released. They've earned her the coveted Amazon author ranking of #1 in Romantic Suspense, Military Romance and Contemporary Romance categories, as well as in Gothic Romance for her Vampires of Tuscany and Guardian Angels. Her characters follow a sometimes rocky road to redemption through passion and true love.

Now that he's out of the Navy, Sharon can share with her readers that her son spent a decade as a Navy SEAL, and he's the inspiration for her books.

Her Golden Vampires of Tuscany are not like any vamps you've read about before, since they don't go to ground and can walk around in the full light of the sun.

Her Guardian Angels struggle with the human charges they are sent to save, often escaping their vanilla world of Heaven for the brief human one. You won't find any of these beings in any Sunday school class.

She lives in Sonoma County, California with her husband and her Doberman, Tucker. A lifelong organic gardener, when she's not writing, she's getting *verra verra* dirty in the mud, or wandering Farmers Markets looking for new Heirloom varieties of vegetables and flowers. She and her husband plan to cure their wanderlust (or make it worse) by traveling in their Diesel Class A Pusher, Romance Rider. Starting with this book, all her writing will be done on the road.

She loves hearing from her fans:
Sharonhamilton2001@gmail.com

Her website is:
sharonhamiltonauthor.com

Find out more about Sharon, her upcoming releases, appearances and news when you sign up for Sharon's newsletter.

Facebook:
facebook.com/SharonHamiltonAuthor

Twitter:
twitter.com/sharonlhamilton

Pinterest:
pinterest.com/AuthorSharonH

Google Plus:
plus.google.com/u/1/+SharonHamiltonAuthor/posts

BookBub:
bookbub.com/authors/sharon-hamilton

Youtube:
youtube.com/channel/UCDInkxXFpXp_4Vnq08ZxMBQ

Soundcloud:
soundcloud.com/sharon-hamilton-1

Sharon Hamilton's Rockin' Romance Readers:
facebook.com/groups/sealteamromance

Sharon Hamilton's Goodreads Group:
goodreads.com/group/show/199125-sharon-hamilton-
readers-group

Visit Sharon's Online Store:
sharon-hamilton-author.myshopify.com

Join Sharon's Review Teams:

eBook Reviews:
sharonhamiltonassistant@gmail.com

Audio Reviews:
sharonhamiltonassistant@gmail.com

Life *is one fool thing after another.*
Love *is two fool things after each other.*

REVIEWS

even finished it up in a day. The vampires in this book were different from your average vampire, but I enjoy different variations and changes to the same old stuff. It made for a more unpredictable read and more adventurous to explore! Vampire lovers, any paranormal readers and even those who love the romance genre will enjoy Honeymoon Bite."

"This is the first non-Seal book of this author's I have read and I loved it. There is a cast-like hierarchy in this vampire community with humans at the very bottom and Golden vampires at the top. Lionel is a dark vampire who are servants of the Goldens. Phoebe is a Golden who has not decided if she will remain human or accept the turning to become a vampire. Either way she and Lionel can never be together since it is forbidden.

I enjoyed this story and I am looking forward to the next installment."

"A hauntingly romantic read. Old love lost and new love found. Family, heart, intrigue and vampires. Grabbed my attention and couldn't put down. Would definitely recommend."

PRAISE FOR THE
SEAL BROTHERHOOD SERIES

"Fans of Navy SEAL romance, I found a new author to feed your addiction. Finely written and loaded delicious with moments, Sharon Hamilton's storytelling satisfies like a thick bar of chocolate." —Marliss Melton, bestselling author of the *Team Twelve* Navy SEALs series

"Sharon Hamilton does an EXCELLENT job of fitting all the characters into a brotherhood of SEALS that may not be real but sure makes you feel that you have entered the circle and security of their world. The stories intertwine with each book before...and each book after and THAT is what makes Sharon Hamilton's SEAL Brotherhood Series so very interesting. You won't want to put down ANY of her books and they will keep you reading into the night when you should be sleeping. Start with this book...and you will not want to stop until you've read the whole series and then...you will be waiting for Sharon to write the next one." (5 Star Review)

"Kyle and Christy explode all over the pages in this first book, *[Accidental SEAL]*, in a whole new series of SEALs. If the twist and turns don't get your heart jumping, then maybe the suspense will. This is a must read for those that are looking for love and adventure with a little sloppy love thrown in for good measure." (5 Star Review)

PRAISE FOR THE
BAD BOYS OF SEAL TEAM 3 SERIES

"I love reading this series! Once you start these books, you can hardly put them down. The mix of romance and suspense keeps you turning the pages one right after another! Can't wait until the next book!" (5 Star Review)

"I love all of Sharon's Seal books, but *[SEAL's Code]* may just be her best to date. Danny and Luci's journey is filled with a wonderful insight into the Native American life. It is a love story that will fill you with warmth and contentment. You will enjoy Danny's journey to become a SEAL and his reasons for it. Good job Sharon!" (5 Star Review)

PRAISE FOR THE
BAND OF BACHELORS SERIES

"*[Lucas]* was the first book in the Band of Bachelors series and it was a phenomenal start. I loved how we got to see the other SEALs we all love and we got a look at Lucas and Marcy. They had an instant attraction, and their love was very intense. This book had it all, suspense, steamy romance, humor, everything you want in a riveting, outstanding read. I can't wait to read the next book in this series." (5 Star Review)

PRAISE FOR THE
TRUE BLUE SEALS SERIES

"Keep the tissues box nearby as you read *True Blue SEALs: Zak* by Sharon Hamilton. I imagine more than I wish to that the circumstances surrounding Zak and Amy are all too real for returning military personnel and their families. Ms. Hamilton has put us right in the middle of struggles and successes that these two high school sweethearts endure. I have read several of Sharon Hamilton's military romances but will say this is the most emotionally intense of the ones that I have read. This is a well-written, realistic story with authentic characters that will have you rooting for them and proud of those who serve to keep us safe. This is an author who writes amazing stories that you love and cry with the characters. Fans of Jessica Scott and Marliss Melton will want to add Sharon Hamilton to their list of realistic military romance writers." (5 Star Review)

AUTHOR'S NOTE

Most of you have read or seen footage of the devastating wildfires that destroyed so much of Sonoma County. We are a resilient community, and while many have moved on to other places, the saying in so many storefronts and schools is "Sonoma Strong."

This story takes place in St. Helena, in Napa County, not Sonoma County. And I use a fictional place called Wet N Wild, a kind of zoo-like game preserve that caters to tourists and adventure seekers, as well as those who just enjoy "glamping."

My story is in no way consistent with the story of Safari West and how the owner saved all his animals. My description of most of how that site is set up and run is entirely fictional. But, one little factoid or detail I did steal from a story I heard by a tour guide. Coyote Smear is a real thing. If you haven't read the book, you'll have to discover for yourself what that means.

Here are some links to articles on the park, for your information.

www.safariwest.com/fires-hope-emerges-video/

abc7news.com/pets-animals/santa-rosas-safari-west-reopens-after-devastating-north-bay-fires/2674986

www.pressdemocrat.com/specialsections/7585721-181/how-the-safari-west-owner?gallery=7525164&sba=AAS

There is also a famous culinary school in Napa, but everything about that school and how it is run, or the celebrity chef program is purely a figment of my own imagination.

This is the last book I will write in my present home. I've been here 35 years. I think it's perfect that the book is about one great adventure. That's what life is, isn't it? So, my next book will be written "on the road." Yes, that Willie Nelson song is playing in my head quite a bit these days. When this book releases, my property will go on its own new adventure with new owners to love and care for it, probably better than I did.

I'm on to the next one!

Love you all, and thank you for loving my books.

Sharon Hamilton
Bennett Valley, California
July 2018

www.ingramcontent.com/pod-product-compliance
Lightning Source LLC
Chambersburg PA
CBHW051423170626
46809CB00006B/2288